She wished for the stars, wished the man she loved loved her

Virginia stared at the full moon and wished with all her heart, but she knew Wilder didn't love anyone. He'd probably never experienced the emotions she was going through now. How sad for both of them.

"Rapunzel, let down your hair." It was Wilder's voice, low and gravelly as the sound of the creek below her. Virginia looked over the side of her deck to the one below and saw him standing there.

"Wrong fairy tale," she said, "I'm not captive and my hair isn't long enough." Her voice was just above a whisper, but her smile couldn't be contained. He'd come home. Wherever Wilder had gone this evening, whoever he'd been with, he'd come home. Alone.

"All right," he said, and was silent for a minute. "Can I offer you a glass of wine, then?"

"That sounds nice," she said, because there was no use denying it. The thought of him being so close— of him entering her room, stepping onto her balcony—was delicious. Forbidden. Wicked. Wonderful.

Virginia wandered back into the bedroom. She probably ought to cover the provocative satin slip she wore with a robe, but she didn't have one. She could change into regular clothes, but… "If it's going to be," she muttered, still not believing her fantasies could come true, "let it be."

SUPER ROMANCE

In 1996 booksellers from across the country voted **Rita Clay Estrada** Best Series Author. Of course, readers have always known that Rita delivers the very best in romance—every one of her seventeen Temptation novels have been winners.

Books by Rita Clay Estrada

Don't miss any of our special offers. Write to us at the following address for information on our newest releases.

Harlequin Reader Service
U.S.: 3010 Walden Ave., P.O. Box 1325, Buffalo, NY 14269
Canadian: P.O. Box 609, Fort Erie, Ont. L2A 5X3

Rita Clay Estrada
WISHES

Harlequin Books

TORONTO • NEW YORK • LONDON
AMSTERDAM • PARIS • SYDNEY • HAMBURG
STOCKHOLM • ATHENS • TOKYO • MILAN
MADRID • WARSAW • BUDAPEST • AUCKLAND

This is for my wonderful aunt,
Virginia Gallagher Steiner, who opened her house to me
every time I ever asked. Thank you. You're great!

And for Diane Levitt, a.k.a. Diane Bernard, my buddy,
fellow critique partner and close sister, who allowed me
to use her beautiful home as the site of this book. I fell in
love with the Lick Creek area, thanks to you.

ISBN 0-373-25734-1

WISHES

Copyright © 1997 by Rita Clay Estrada.

1

READING WAS A HABIT that had to be fed. Virginia Gallagher shifted the load of newly bought books so the straps of her canvas bag wouldn't cut into her shoulder. Anticipating an evening's readathon, she left the bookstore and headed for her car—a fat little eighteen-year-old Volkswagen. Obviously her jalopy had once been bright yellow and had seen much better days. Still, when Virginia had picked it out in the used-car lot, it had looked a hundred—a thousand—times better than taking the bus in this city.

Chastising herself for spending too much money on books today, she placed the bag in the front passenger seat and walked around the car. When her toe hit something she stopped.

Lying on the tarmac just inches from the tip of her sneaker was a ladies leather wallet. It looked expensive. And fat. Virginia looked around the large parking lot. There were only a few people milling about, and none looked as if they'd come from this direction. The parking space beside her was empty, but it seemed logical that whoever had been there earlier had dropped it from the passenger side. She vaguely remembered a cream-colored Mercedes sedan pulling in next to her just as she was locking the car but it was gone now without a trace. It certainly hadn't left an oil slick like the one that would be shining on the pavement when *she* pulled out.

She picked up the wallet, waiting for someone to tap her on the shoulder and demand it back. When nothing happened, she looked inside. The Texas driver's license tucked in a plastic window depicted an older woman who looked like someone's sweet grandmother. She had gray-blond hair, a wrinkled smile and dimples that, years ago, must have stopped the men of her generation dead in their tracks, perhaps still did.

The address caught her eye. The woman lived outside of Austin, in the hill country, just a few miles from the prestigious Lake Travis community and not far from the Willie Nelson compound. It was a beautiful, rugged area, although most people wouldn't move there because water was scarce in that part of the Edwards Plateau. Those who did live there usually had a lot of acres and a lot of money.

Under the flap of the billfold was tucked a wad of dull green bills—a wad of twenties and fifties neatly piled together, all with heads of famous presidents carefully placed to face the same direction.

Virginia broke out in a sweat. She had in her hand lots and lots of money. She snapped the wallet closed and opened the dented door of her old Volkswagen. Then, in the privacy of the interior, she began counting. Her face grew warmer and warmer until—one thousand twenty dollars later—she was certain she was having the kind of hot flash that Sadie in the diner was always talking about.

One thousand dollars! One thousand individual reasons why life was good!

Stop, she warned herself. This wasn't hers. If she was the woman she thought she was, she wouldn't even *think* about this being her money.

With rigid determination, she dropped the wallet into her purse and slipped the keys into the ignition. It was time to get home and call the owner. Maybe, if she was lucky, Mrs. Ila Hunnicut would give her a reward. Even fifty dollars seemed like a fortune right now.

Virginia could hear her mother—God rest her soul— now. "It's not enough to do the right thing. You should be doing the right thing for the right reasons."

Virginia and her two younger sisters, Elizabeth and Mary, had heard that sentiment often enough growing up. Their mother had been full of life's little lessons, and though she was gone, the advice and support she had always given lingered. Which was a problem, because that icky moral fiber stuck in some way or another to each one of them. All three Gallagher girls, although off pursuing their own dreams, had been bred with a set of standards that didn't always harmonize with the rest of the world.

That was the way of things, though Virginia and her sisters, although not quite achieving what they wanted, hadn't done so badly. They'd get where they were going on their own and be proud because of it.

And until another way of life proved better, they would continue to follow their mother's advice.

But it was okay to dream. There was no harm in that. After all, people who played the lottery dreamed with every ticket they bought....

What if she kept the money? Virginia mused. What would she do with it? As many ideas came to mind as dollars were in the wallet.

She would pay her apartment rent in advance so she wouldn't have to worry about scraping by for the next four months.

She would buy a dress—she hadn't had anything new in over two years—and she'd get a real, professional haircut. Then she'd pay the rest of her bills.

She would get the air-conditioning in her car fixed so she wouldn't have to swelter anymore.

She would pay off her tuition so there wouldn't be any more loans to pay after she graduated from this— her last—year of cooking school.

She would buy a ticket to visit her sisters. She hadn't seen them in three years and missed them so much....

As she wound through the streets of Austin to her small flat in an old house on the south side of the downtown area, the imaginary list continued to grow.

By the time she'd pulled onto her street, she'd satisfied herself that it was fun to dream, but a thousand dollars wasn't enough to change the next four months that much. Besides, she knew she couldn't live with her guilty conscience if she didn't turn over the wallet.

She was tempted to change her mind when she

reached her two-room, third-floor loft apartment. Picking up the phone to dial the number she'd found tucked behind the driver's license, she was greeted with no sound at all. She clicked the button once, twice. She checked the wires to make sure they were connected properly. And then she knew. Her phone had been cut off. Again. She'd forgotten to pay the bill. Forgotten? Heck, she'd run out of money, and it had come down to paying either the electricity or the phone. She'd hoped the phone company would be patient and wait a week, but obviously that hadn't been the case.

Her good intentions had been foiled by lack of funds to back them up. She sighed and plopped into her upholstered, thrift-shop chair. The stuffing popped out of a small tear and the cotton clung to her sleeve. She absently wiped it off as she thought.

Her paycheck from waitressing at the diner would put the phone in working order, but she wouldn't receive it until Monday morning.

She looked at the small stack of books she'd bought this morning. It wouldn't do any good to take them back—they already came from a used-book store, and they'd been on the sale table to boot. Besides, she could do anything—survive fires, floods and near famines—as long as she had books to read. At this point, her six-dollar-a-week addiction was nothing.

Virginia made herself a cup of green tea, curled up in her overstuffed chair and reached for the first book on the stack. It was six o'clock on a Saturday evening.

She had just come off a twelve-hour shift at the

diner, so she didn't have to go to work until Sunday afternoon. She didn't have to go back to school until Monday morning. She couldn't phone about the overstuffed wallet she'd found until tomorrow at work.

Virginia gave a happy sigh. It was her time. She could read until she fell asleep.

WHEN VIRGINIA ARRIVED at work late Sunday afternoon, there was a bounce in her step. She'd done nothing but read and sleep for almost a day, and it felt as if she'd had a week's vacation.

Although the Sunrise Diner hadn't changed much in several decades, it was an "in" spot to go for a lunch or dinner and to indulge in nostalgia for the fifties. Even on Sunday, the place was noisy with tourists and a sprinkling of government workers.

Quarter in hand, Virginia made her way to the pay phone. In her other hand was the phone number of the wallet's owner. It was time to put the woman out of her misery. Virginia got sidetracked when Sadie, one of the waitresses, called to her.

"Hey, Ginny! Grab order 101, will you? It goes to table 14."

With a resigned shrug, Virginia did as she was asked. It wasn't fair to make a customer wait. As soon as she delivered the order, she went back to the phone, dialed the number and waited impatiently for someone to answer.

When she heard a female voice on the line, she sighed in relief. "Is Mrs. Hunnicut there?"

"Who shall I say is calling?" the woman requested formally.

"This is Virginia Gallagher, and I believe I found something that belongs to Mrs. Hunnicut."

"Just a moment, please."

Virginia waited impatiently; Sadie was hollering again, but this time Virginia ignored her. Even though she had intended to do the right thing from the start, the wallet was burning a hole in her purse and she felt like a thief. She fully expected the law to lay a heavy hand on her shoulder and ask the whereabouts of Mrs. Hunnicut's money.

"This is Mrs. Hunnicut speaking," announced a friendly, slightly quavery voice.

"Mrs. Hunnicut, you don't know me, but my name is Virginia and I found something of yours."

"My wallet?" the woman asked.

Virginia sighed in relief. "Yes, ma'am," she said. "And I wanted to return it to you."

"Well, my goodness, that's *wonderful* news, isn't it?"

The woman sounded so cheery Virginia had to laugh. "I hope so. I would imagine it'd be hard to replace some of the contents."

"What is your full name, dear?"

"Virginia Gallagher."

"What a lovely name. It hints of fairies and legends and lore."

"Thank you." Virginia brushed off the compliment, not wanting to stray from the topic of giving back the money. "How can I get this to you? Or would you like to come by and pick it up? I work in town on Sixth Street."

"What color is your hair?"

Virginia automatically touched a strand of thick hair resting on her shoulder. "My hair? It's blond—strawberry blond, actually."

"How extraordinary. I tell you what," the older woman said conspiratorially. "My son drives by Sixth Street every evening on his way home. He could pick you up and bring you along some night. I want to meet such a sweet young person who is so honest she wants to rid herself of a fat wallet before it weighs on her."

Virginia grinned. The woman had read her correctly. "That's fine, but I can just hand this over to your son and he can bring it to you."

"Indulge me," Mrs. Hunnicut prompted. "I want to meet you and give you a reward—a small token of my esteem."

"Well, okay," Virginia said, her mind racing ahead, mentally checking her schedule. "But I can't make it for a day or so."

They discussed a day and time, then settled on Wednesday evening after she finished her shift at the restaurant.

"My son will pick you up," Mrs. Hunnicut said, a distinct touch of humor in her voice. "You'll know him by his Brooks Brothers suit and uptight ways. But aside from that, he'll be the most handsome man in the restaurant. He's very nice. Really."

Virginia laughed. Nothing like a proud mama. "I'm

sure I won't miss him," she said before hanging up. But it wouldn't be because of his handsomeness or the smile on his face—it'd be his Brooks Brothers suit. Not that many came in the door of the diner. Even though Austin was the state capital, the chances of one of the wealthy congressmen dressed in that brand of suit eating here was slim to none. They would most probably go somewhere more upscale. There were plenty of other, more formal places to dine. This was where the average political worker and man-on-the-street came to get his money's worth. Takeout abounded. The food was good, fast and hefty in calories.

Sadie thrust a tray full of food into Virginia's hand. "Come in late and you take what God gives you," she said hurriedly. "Booth 11 needs this now."

"I wasn't late. I was early." But Virginia was talking to the air. Sadie was walking away so fast it looked as if she was trotting. Virginia noticed a decided limp in her fellow worker's gait as she hurried to the counter to pick up the next order. Her feet must be hurting again. Sadie had worked in the diner for over fifteen years, beginning because she had to support three little kids whose father had walked out on them. But the children were grown now, and Sadie was still here. The owner, Tally, had promised her a small portion of the overall business as a pension if she stayed on and kept the serving staff in order.

Virginia took the food to the table and smiled as she delivered it. Four more months and she'd be doing the cooking, not the serving, only she wouldn't be cooking in a diner. No, she would be chef in some wonderful, chic restaurant where food was entertainment, not survival or necessity. And after that, she'd become her own boss. Destiny would be hers—and so would money. Finally.

She worked hard all afternoon; it wasn't until a little after four o'clock that she was able to take a break. If she was lucky, she'd be out by four-thirty anyway. She walked out the back door of the restaurant, sat on one of the wooden boxes piled there and took a deep, heavy breath. Then, leaning back against the ancient wood of the building, she propped her aching feet up on another box and tilted her face toward the last of the afternoon sun. A few minutes later, Sadie joined her.

"It's been hectic all day today," Sadie complained in her gravelly voice, reaching in the pocket of her stained apron for an unfiltered cigarette. A click of a lighter later, Virginia heard her wheeze as she inhaled tobacco smoke. "Everybody wanted great diner food today instead of those fancy watercress-and-cucumber sandwiches," Sadie added, just as she had a million other times when the diner was busier than usual.

"Looks like it," Virginia muttered, stifling a yawn.

"What was so important you had to make a phone call when you got here?"

"I found a wallet yesterday."

"Really? With money in it?" Sadie's voice was full of interest.

"With money," she confirmed. "And I had to call the owner. My phone isn't working."

"You forgot to pay the bill again."

"I didn't have money to pay the bill," Virginia corrected. "The last two weeks' tips were worse than ever. Thank goodness legislature is in session again or I'd be pounding the pavement looking for another job."

"Don't worry," Sadie said, patting Virginia's knee. "You'll be out of school on the other side of the counter soon enough. I still don't know why you don't help Tally out right now."

"Because I'm not cooking the same food he makes. My specialty is Southwest cooking, not meat loaf and instant potatoes with canned gravy. Besides, right now it's easier to serve than to think about cooking after being in school and cooking all day."

"Take it easy, honey. You're coming to the end of this road. It's taken two years, but it was worth it. You deserve better and you'll get there. And when you do, I'll retire and oversee your place, just to keep my hand in." Sadie's words were a repeat of what she'd said before. In fact, the whole conversation was a repeat, familiar banter to reinforce their belief that there would be a better time for them both.

Virginia hoped so. Right now she was so tired of her schedule that she'd chuck it for a quarter and a one-way ticket to some deserted Caribbean island where she'd have to fish for her food and drink coconut milk....

Monday and Tuesday were hectic, too. Virginia went to school, came home and transcribed her notes on nutrition, tried a few new recipes and collapsed. By Wednesday she was ready for a day of routine.

Once more she worked with Sadie, and once more she took a late break.

"Is today the big day?" Sadie asked, puffing on her cigarette.

"Yes. The son is coming to pick me up and take me to his mother's. I'll be dining there, then they'll take me home."

"*Dining!*" Sadie exclaimed with a hoity-toity accent. "My, my, we're fancy."

"Hey, Virginia!" Tally called. "Git on in here, doll-face. There's somebody here for you."

Her eyes popped open. "Good grief, he's here!"

"Who?"

"Mrs. Hunnicut's son." Virginia stood up and brushed her pants free of sawdust.

"Mrs. Hunnicut?" Sadie said, awe and disbelief in her voice. "Mother of *Wilder* Hunnicut? Ace Computers' founder?"

That stopped Virginia in her tracks. "Is that who it is?"

"I would guess so. Her son runs one of the up-and-coming companies in the country and you found her wallet? Lucky you." Sadie tilted her head thoughtfully. "That's great. Maybe they'll give you a hefty reward and you won't have to worry about money for a while."

"And maybe they'll just give me a boot and tell me to go on my way," Virginia muttered, but her mind was suddenly full of possibilities. Maybe, just maybe, she'd get enough to help with next week's electricity bill. Wouldn't that be nice? After all, she supposed she deserved some kind of reward for her honesty. Even fifty dollars would help at this point; a hundred would be like heaven.

All logical thought ceased as she walked into the diner and Tally pointed his spatula at a man sitting in the corner of the diner reading a financial newspaper. He was dressed in a gray suit, and though Virginia wouldn't know the difference, she was pretty sure it was a Brooks Brothers suit. If fabric and cut were anything to judge by, it was very expensive, that much was certain. He wore a power tie in red and yellow and a pale yellow dress shirt that had to be silk. And this one covered a body that looked lean and muscular, with a broad back, strong arms, thick neck.

The most arresting thing about him, though, was his face. It was long and tanned with a decidedly square jaw, a straight nose and high cheekbones. His thick, dark blond hair had a smattering of gray at the temples and was cut to perfection. *Handsome* wasn't the only word that came to mind.

Imposing.

Regal.

Charismatic.

Those words and more tumbled about in her brain. Virginia walked over to him and stood for a minute. When he didn't notice her, she cleared her throat. Still he didn't look up.

"Uh, Mr. Hunnicut?"

The gentleman raised one well-manicured finger. "Just a moment, please."

The noise of dishes being stacked and pots and pans being scraped and scrubbed filled the silence between them.

Virginia waited as he took out his pen and circled one of the stock quotes—she couldn't see which one. Then he put the cap on his pen and pocketed it.

His hazel-eyed gaze was riveting. "Yes, I'm Wilder Hunnicut."

She remembered where she was and what she was supposed to be accomplishing. "I'm Virginia Gallagher?" she prompted. He still looked blank. "I found your mother's wallet?"

Recognition suddenly shone in his eyes. "Oh, yes. Of course." His apologetic smile—deep-slashed dimples and all—was enough to light up the room. She was reminded of his mother's picture. "I'm sorry. I was in the middle of a thought."

"I understand."

"I have a tendency to focus on things and lose track of the people around me."

Virginia returned his smile. "It's probably very necessary in order to head up a company such as yours."

His brows rose. "You're familiar with Ace Corporation?"

"I'm familiar with your computers. They're the second-biggest seller in the country," she stated quietly.

"Don't repeat that to anyone. My stockholders think we're number one."

Virginia looked innocently amazed. "Really? Don't they read the *Wall Street Journal*?"

It took him only a second or two before his smile turned to deep, rich laughter.

She felt great satisfaction at having caught him off guard enough to laugh. She had a feeling he didn't do it often enough. Besides, the slash-mark dimples were a great reward. "Sorry. Couldn't resist."

Wilder Hunnicut folded his paper and stood. "Smart girl. Do you read the *Journal* often?"

"Often enough. We have a few customers who read it and leave it here when they go back to work. I take it home and see if there's anything I can do to earn more money."

Wilder Hunnicut looked incredulous. "In the stock market?"

She nodded. "I own ten shares of your stock, you know."

"Ten shares?"

"Yes. I bought them through an investment club but haven't been able to add to them yet. I will soon, though. Meanwhile my dividends are going toward more partial shares of stock." She knew her voice held a note of pride. She'd made the decision to add a dollar a week to the small inheritance her mother had left each of her daughters. Virginia's two sisters had chosen other stocks but she'd decided to invest in the up-and-coming Texas-owned computer company.

"Smart investment. How long have you had them?"

"About three years. I've needed money often enough during that period, but I'm not selling them. Ever. They'll be my nest egg in my old age."

"I think you'll need more than ten shares to take care of you in your old age."

"Maybe. But it's a start," she stated coolly. He didn't need to denigrate her piddling savings. It was more than some had. "How many shares did you own when you were my age?"

His grin was patronizing. "A few more than that."

"And how many did you buy on your own with money you made without family help?"

"I see your point." Wilder Hunnicut narrowed his hazel-eyed gaze and drawled, "The lady has fangs."

Virginia tilted her chin upward at a determined angle. "Wrong again. The lady has *pride*. My stock was honestly earned and so was my pride in earning it."

He slipped the paper under his arm. "Congratulations. So was mine." His hazel eyes were cool. "Are you ready to go?"

Obviously he thought she wasn't worthy of further conversation. "Of course. Let me get my purse."

"I'll wait outside. The maroon, double-parked van is mine. Come out when you're ready."

"Van?"

"It's easier for business." Mr. Wilder Hunnicut walked out the door without a backward glance.

She watched him go, stunned that he would be so

rude to someone—anyone—let alone the woman who was returning his mother's money.

Virginia walked into the storage room where lockers lined one wall. With a flick and a couple of twists, she opened her combination lock and took out a neatly folded pair of coffee brown pants and a matching sweater. With economic movements, she stripped and redressed in a matter of minutes. She was not going to dine with the Hunnicuts wearing a waitress uniform. Even if it was just pants, it was much better than anything else she owned, and good enough to make a decent impression. So it wasn't a dress—she wasn't part of their world.

With a few strokes of a brush through her hair, a dab of blush, a touch of peach-tinted lip gloss and a swipe of mascara, she was presentable. Almost. She reached inside her purse and pulled out a bottle of her favorite tea-rose perfume wrapped in paper towels. She only wore it on special occasions; it was a little too pricey for everyday use.

She stuffed her uniform back in the locker, grabbed her purse and waved goodbye as she ran out the front door. The van was indeed double-parked at the curb.

A young man in a dark suit who looked more like a college student than a colleague of Wilder Hunnicut stood just outside the sliding side door, leisurely talking to someone seated inside. When he saw her, he straightened, his smile widening as he watched her approach. "Ms. Gallagher?"

Her gaze darted to the van's open door, but she

couldn't see much of anything or anyone. She looked back at the young man who was apparently the driver. Everything showed on his fresh face, including his enthusiasm for his job. "Yes?"

With a slight flourish he gestured toward the steps just below the door. "This way, please, ma'am."

Ma'am? She wasn't old enough to be called ma'am, was she? He was only a little younger than her! With a feeling of impending age, she stepped inside the vehicle. It wasn't what she'd expected at all.

The roof of this van was much higher than average, enabling her to stand erect. The rest of the vehicle had also been customized. It held three comfortable captain's chairs, with a desk in front of one of them. A one-drawer filing cabinet sat between the other two chairs and did double duty as a low cocktail table. A small TV screen was hung behind the driver's seat, attached to the Plexiglas that divided the office area from the front.

"An office?" she asked with raised eyebrows.

Wilder Hunnicut leaned back in his executive seat and smiled at her. "It's a forty-five minute drive home without traffic jams. Having this mobile office means I get an extra two hours of work done a day. It pays for itself."

"How plush," she murmured, looking around at the rest of her surroundings. "How efficient."

"Would you like a glass of wine?" he asked cordially. The paper he'd been reading in the restaurant was neatly folded to expose the stock-market quotes; the computer on his desk was running a program that looked as if it tracked certain stocks and prices. He certainly took his travel time seriously.

"No, thank you," she said primly, not wanting to take him away from all that. Readjusting her seat she tried to act as if she rode in a van like this every day of the week.

The driver put the car in gear, and as they drove down the street Virginia saw Sadie standing at the diner window watching them. She was probably wondering if Virginia was in the right car. She would have expected the owner of Ace Corporation to drive a Porsche, or at least have a stretch limousine.

"Who would have thought?" Virginia murmured.

"The van?" Wilder chuckled. "It's the perfect solution for me. I can get caught up on my reading or stare out the window or concentrate on a project with the PC." He gestured to the laptop on his desk. "It interfaces with both my home and office computers."

"Of course."

He grinned. "Of course."

"No interruptions," she added, counting up the advantages he hadn't mentioned.

The cell phone rang and he reached into his coat pocket and pulled it out. Flipping down the speaker, he said, "*Almost* none."

In the first moment, Virginia could tell it was his mother calling. "Yes, I just picked her up and we're on our way. Yes. Yes. Yes. No. Talk to you when we get there." He hesitated a moment. "Right."

"Mothers can track you down anywhere," Virginia said, a twinkle in her eye. "I think it's a genetic thing."

"That, and the fact that she's one of only three people I've given this number to."

"Doesn't matter. Even if you hadn't given it to her, your mother would have tracked you down."

His husky laugh filled the air. "You're right. Sometimes I think her instinct is so well honed she started developing it before I was even born." He shook his head ruefully and replaced the phone. "I keep thinking I must have had an older sibling she practiced on before I came along. But alas, there's no one in front of me, forging the way."

Virginia nodded as the obvious hit her. "You're an only child," she stated.

"How did you guess?"

"Overachiever." She nodded sagely. "That was the giveaway."

He laughed. "And you?"

"I'm the oldest of three girls, raised in an Irish Catholic community in the North."

"Wow." He gave a low whistle between his teeth. "And I thought being an only child was bad."

"At least you're a Texan by birth."

"Instead of by choice?"

She laughed. "By birth is a definite advantage if you live in Texas."

She leaned back, remembering her own childhood days as if they were yesterday. "It was wonderful growing up there, but I'm glad I'm here now. Don't think I didn't love my family," she hastened to add. "We may be scattered around the countryside now, but when we were growing up together, we were tight. One or the other of us would always play the moving target. That kept mom from focusing on any one of us."

Wilder smiled. "It sounds like fun. As an only child, I didn't have that team spirit. We lived out in the country, so I didn't even have neighborhood kids that I was close to."

"In those days everybody minded everybody else's business when it came to the children. My first year in high school my dad died, but we had a dozen fathers and mothers who kept an eagle eye on our activities outside our apartment."

"Where was this?"

"Mount Clemens, Michigan."

He looked startled. "Texas is a long way from there. How did you end up in Austin?"

"I came down with two other friends. They've moved on, but not me." She grinned. "I saw the bright lights and knew I'd found home."

"And your sisters? Are you the only one who left home?"

"Good grief, no. Elizabeth Jean is in Atlanta working with teenage single mothers. Mary Ellen is chasing her dream; she runs a small video business outside of Chicago. In another two years it'll be all hers."

"And what about you? What do you want to do?"

"I've worked for years toward becoming a chef. I've

got four months to go before I graduate from a cooking school specializing in Southwest cuisine. One of the best chefs in the country teaches there every other year. And this is the year."

"When you're through? What then?" Wilder prompted. His hazel eyes bore into hers until she felt the heat of a flush begin somewhere around her toes and work its way up to her cheeks.

She swallowed and looked around the van, then out the window at passing traffic—anywhere but at him. Still, that heat was building. "We'll see. A fancy restaurant somewhere will hire me as apprentice chef and then, soon, I'll become a world-class chef in my field. Then I'll write books, do world tours and in general be the success that it's my destiny to be."

"Of course," he stated dryly, as if her dream was inconsequential and could be brushed off. She was glad. It really *was* her dream, but she'd rather pass it off as silly than have someone outside the business comment on her vulnerabilities.

"Of course," she repeated. "But if it doesn't happen exactly that way, I'll still be a success."

"It all depends on the meaning of the word *success*, doesn't it?" he asked, his patronizing attitude right back on track.

"It certainly does," Virginia agreed. "And the meaning has to be important to me—not to you."

Wilder grimaced. "Ouch. Touché."

Her voice was laced with satisfaction. "Sorry."

He stared at her a moment, but she refused to look at

him. Instead, she gazed out the side window and tried to see if there were any landmarks she recognized. There were none.

Wilder gave a sigh, then turned to the keyboard and began to work, watching the screen as intently as he'd been watching her earlier.

Virginia relaxed, relieved to be out from under the microscope. She had a feeling that not much escaped Wilder Hunnicut's attention when he wanted to zero in. That's probably why he was such a winner in his own line of business. It wasn't his fault he didn't realize that success didn't always equate with money.

But it was truce time. They had to be nearing the Hunnicut home. Soon he could hand her over to his mother, who could do the honors of receiving her wallet back and giving Virginia her dues. She only hoped the reward was more than just dinner; her unpaid phone bill came instantly to mind.

She'd bet her last $17.80 that Wilder Hunnicut didn't have to worry about paying *his* phone bill.

2

THE VAN SLOWED, then turned off the main highway, swinging onto a small road that ran beside a rushing creek. The road widened as it jogged away from the streambed. They drove through another gate, then began a decent around a steep hill. At last Virginia saw where they were headed.

In front of them was a house reminiscent of the mission at the Alamo. Its warm, peach-colored stucco reflected the last of the evening sun peeping over the hill. Not until they pulled around to the side entrance, where the doors to a three-car garage sat open, did Virginia realize the house was multistoried. There were many levels built into the cliff, affording each a stunning view of the valley below.

"Lord," Virginia whispered. "It's outrageous."

Wilder laughed. "Wait till you see the rest."

They left the van and walked down the stone pathway to huge double doors carved out of wood. Virginia figured they had to be twelve feet high.

"They came from an old mission in Mexico," Wilder stated before she could ask. "So did Michael the Archangel." He pointed directly above the door, where a six-foot-tall, winged angel, carved from the same wood, guarded the entrance.

When Wilder opened the door, Virginia stepped into the terra-cotta-tiled entry. The large square area was decorated with wonderful turn-of-the-century photos of Mexican *bandidos* surrounded by their women and children. Interspersed with them were subtle paintings of colonial Mexico, where the French had taken up court in Napoleon's time.

The sound of a tapping cane reached her ears, grew louder. "Wilder? Is that you?" Virginia recognized Mrs. Hunnicut's voice from the phone.

"Yes, Mom. And I brought Ms. Gallagher with me."

A spritely older woman with a crown of blond-gold hair came into view, a smile lighting her eyes. "Good, now I have someone to talk to this evening who won't be quoting me stock prices."

"I thought you liked my business conversation," Wilder said, but his humor matched his mother's. "You always said you learned so much."

"Oh, bosh, Wilder. You know better. It was just your way of getting back at me for reading you those 'ridiculous fairy tales' you hated so much as a child." The older woman finally turned her gaze on Virginia. Her hazel eyes had lost some of their color to age, but the mirth there was as youthful as ever, Virginia was sure. Mrs. Hunnicut openly looked her up and down, Virginia stared back. Then pronounced with satisfaction, "What a wonderful smile," as she held out her hand. "So you are Virginia."

"I am," she said, pulling her purse off her shoulder to reach for the wallet inside. "And I have something for you."

Mrs. Hunnicut patted her hand. "Hold it for a while, dear. I'm sure you won't forget to leave it before Sammy drives you home." She linked her arm to Virginia's and led her through an open-concept dining room, into a triangular great room. In the center of the triangle was a fireplace, on either side of which rose walls of glass reaching the cathedral ceiling. French doors at either end opened to the natural-wood deck that wrapped around the building.

All the while, the older woman chattered away. "This is really my son's home. Mine is far more formal, but I've been here for the past six months, recovering from a mild stroke. As much as I love the boy, his idea of home is something that looks as if he built walls around the Sahara."

Virginia looked about appreciatively. Soft desert colors accented by a deep forest green, sharp and curved nooks and crannies created by walls of glass brought the outside directly into the living and dining rooms. And the view was truly spectacular. Virginia felt as if she was perched on the edge of a small Grand Canyon. Across from the house was a slightly higher cliff than the one where they were perched; time and water had cut through the earth's strata, exposing into a vivid portrait of millennia. Grays mixed with dark reds and pale tans, one layer over another until, at the top, the shrubs and trees of the hill country added green.

Virginia moved to the window, drawn by the unsurpassed beauty of the scene. As she reached the glass, she realized that the vented windows on each side let in the breeze and the sounds of nature. Her breath caught in her throat as she stared down. On the bottom of the limestone bed crystal-clear water rushed over white and gray rocks, gurgling merrily as it ran past the house.

"How wonderful," she whispered, unaware she'd spoken out loud.

"It is, isn't it?" replied Mrs. Hunnicut. "It's my favorite sound. I'm not sure, but I think I might visit my son far less frequently if his home was anywhere else."

"Now she tells me," Wilder stated dryly, but the playful gleam in his eye gave him away. He was as delighted with his mother's company as his mother was by his. They seemed to be two strong individuals who had learned to compromise for the sake of their relationship. Virginia felt a stab of envy, but she brushed it quickly away.

Wilder stood next to her, offering a long-stemmed crystal glass. "Wine?"

She took the glass and smiled up into his hazel eyes. "Thanks," she said, hoping her voice didn't reveal the warmth that suffused her body.

He handed a glass of wine to his mother, who sipped delicately and said, "Good choice, Wilder." Obviously they were both knowledgeable about fine wine.

And Virginia was not. She imagined there were several hundred other things she didn't know that, in their everyday life, the Hunnicuts took for granted. It made her feel like the country mouse come to tea. But there was a part of her that craved to know—to actually live this way. In fact, this evening was the opportunity of a lifetime. Her friends would be awed and amazed that she'd stood in the home of the famous Wilder Hunnicut, sipping fine wine and discussing the stupendous view while waiting for a sumptuous dinner to be served. She might never pass this way again.

She decided that she might as well accept this journey for what it was, and enjoy being one of them, if just for a moment.

Virginia smiled and turned to Wilder. "This is delicious. Thank you."

Wilder's hazel eyes were on her, and she felt herself warm again under his gaze. "You're quite welcome," he said.

Mrs. Hunnicut sat down on the forest green, leather sofa and patted the seat next to her. "Come sit next to me, dear, and tell me about yourself. Do you come from Austin?"

Virginia made her history as brief as possible, knowing that, although Wilder averted his gaze to the sunset, he was listening to this story—again.

"...And so here I am," she finished simply.

"You say you found my wallet. If I remember correctly, there was a bookstore in that shopping center. Are you a reader of fiction?"

The older woman's question surprised Virginia.

There were so many other things she could have asked. "Yes. It's my escape. I'm not into watching television."

"That's wonderful. I'm a reader myself." Mrs. Hunnicut sighed. "The wonderful thing is that you can take a book with you wherever you go. You can't do that with one of those TVs."

"An age-old argument," Wilder murmured. "Mother believes that I should advertise my computers in books instead of on TV. She doesn't see any benefit in television. She says 'thinking people' use computers."

Virginia looked at mother and son. "I thought thinking people thought. It didn't dawn on me that they thought only one way," she mused.

Laughter from the two Hunnicuts echoed in the evening air. At first Virginia thought they were laughing at her, until she realized their expressions were both delighted and indulgent.

"You're absolutely right, my dear," the older woman said, with a pat on her hand. "Wisdom comes easily to some, while others are buried in their own mired way of thinking."

"I didn't mean..."

Mrs. Hunnicut's smile was as rueful as Wilder's grin was satisfied. "It was meant well, and that's all that counts." She glanced at her son. "Stop grinning like a Cheshire cat and fill my glass, Wilder, or I shall tell Virginia what a wayward child you are."

The owner of the second-largest computer company in the country was a wayward child? Virginia hardly thought so. "I meant that thinking people are open to all forms of advertisement," she said. "Why limit the source? It seems to me that it's not that much different from advertising a restaurant."

Wilder lost his smile. "Perhaps." She'd insulted him somehow.

"How bright you are, child. Just the sort of woman to find a wallet and bring it back to its rightful owner."

"Wasn't that lucky?" Wilder sounded distant and he turned his back on both women to stare out at the striking view of the water.

Virginia reached into her purse and pulled out the wallet. "Speaking of which..." she said, only relaxing when the other woman took it. "I'm glad to get that out of my hands."

Mrs. Hunnicut stared down at the unopened wallet in her lap. "Most people would have loved to find this. They'd probably have taken the money and run." She looked back at Virginia, her gaze piercing. "Why didn't you?"

Virginia shook her head. "Like the kids say, 'it's not my style, man.' I've never taken anything since I was seven and the clerk in a drugstore caught me stealing a candy bar. I was humiliated beyond belief and vowed never to put myself in that position again." She grinned at the memory of the episode.

"I wish all lessons were so easily learned," Mrs. Hunnicut stated with a sigh.

Just then a middle-aged woman appeared at the doorway. "Ma'am? Dinner is served."

"Wonderful, Maggie. Thank you." She turned back to Virginia, her pleasure apparent. "We get to have my son sit with us for a little while before he rushes off." Mrs. Hunnicut stood. Leaning heavily on her cane, she walked slowly toward the dining area. "It's a rare thing when he's home this long in the early evening. Usually there are sixteen charity events requiring his presence, and a hundred and sixteen women pounding on the door or phoning to get his attention."

"An exaggeration if I ever heard one," Wilder stated, unperturbed at his mother's accusation. "Twenty or thirty, maybe. But that's the limit."

Laughter spilled from Virginia's lips before she could stop it. "Do you two spar often?" she finally managed to say.

"Every time we're together. Isn't that true, dear?" Mrs. Hunnicut said as Wilder pulled out a chair for her at the end of the table.

"Too often true," Wilder said, motioning for Virginia to sit at the other end. When she hesitated, he motioned again. She'd obviously been forgiven. "I'd rather sit between two women than be left out at one end of the table." He grinned, and Virginia felt her insides melt at the pure, raw sexiness of him.

Immediately, she did as she was told, sitting primly in the seat that was normally reserved for the man of the house. It felt good to be there. She sat a little straighter, feeling worthy of any man's place. She'd been striving to enter a career that was mainly occupied and controlled by men—the great chefs of America and Europe were mostly male. If she was equal to them, she was certainly equal to heading the table in the home of one of the country's greatest computer gurus.

"I have a feeling that whatever thoughts just filtered through your mind were not in my favor," he murmured, sitting down. It seemed he'd been watching the expressions flit across her face.

"I was just thinking that I was up to the challenge of sitting at the head of the table," she told him with a teasing grin.

"Quite so, my dear," Mrs. Hunnicut said calmly with a snap of her napkin.

Virginia followed suit.

"I know when I'm outmaneuvered," Wilder murmured, placing his own napkin in his lap.

Dinner conversation was light and wonderful and heady. Even though Virginia paid close attention to the menu and its preparation, most of her concentration was on the sexy man seated between her and Mrs. Hunnicut. Wilder's winsome smile, his sharp wit and wonderful sense of humor were all aphrodisiacs. Even the way he treated his mother, who was a doll, in Virginia's estimation, gave her a warm, wonderful feeling in the pit of her stomach that had nothing to do with delicious food or fine wine.

She forced herself to concentrate on the meal, attempting to guess what spices the chef had used, but with Wilder so close and his fascination so great, it was difficult.

The doorbell chimed, but didn't interrupt the conversation. Mrs. Hunnicut continued her telling of a funny story about a friend who, at eighty-nine, still played bridge twice a week—and drove to every game, much to the chagrin of her friends and family.

Suddenly, from the doorway, came a female voice.

"Hello, everyone." Virginia looked over to see a stately, beautiful blonde in a short, tight blue dress she wore with the panache of an haute-couture model.

Virginia was stung by something she didn't want to name or to know.

"Hello, Greta," Wilder said smoothly, his fingers stroking the stem of his wineglass. "I must have forgotten the time."

"I'm just a touch early, darling. I came off a shoot by noon and had a nice, long nap." She smiled. "I'm ready to dance all night."

"With anyone in particular?"

Greta pouted, but it was all in fun. "Don't press your luck, Wilder, or I'll tell everyone you secretly write country-and-western lyrics. The ones that say you lost your house, your car and your woman."

"If I were to succeed as a country-music songwriter I have a feeling it might be a little easier on me than following the path I've chosen."

"Party pooper."

Mrs. Hunnicut gave a hefty sigh. Virginia realized that the older woman was a sighing expert. From the look on Wilder's face, he knew it, too, and heard whole sentences in that sound. But it didn't seem to bother him.

"Have a nice evening, Mother," he said, kissing the top of her head. "Don't wait up."

"Not likely," Mrs. Hunnicut muttered. "You lead a wild life, son."

"Not wild enough, Mrs. Hunnicut," Greta chirped over her shoulder as she and Wilder walked arm-in-arm toward the door.

Virginia watched them leave with envy growing in her heart. When had she had *her* last date? Three months ago? Four? All right, so maybe it was a year ago. She and some guy named John had gone to a movie, then grabbed a hamburger. He'd told her how wonderful it was to be with her, after having discovered his wife was dating a cross-dresser. It had been a memorable date, but not one of Virginia's finest.

Other thoughts crowded her mind. Would she ever date again? Although there wasn't time in her life for a romance right now, she hoped there was a man out there for her. In a couple-oriented society, she sometimes felt like an oddity.

It wasn't that she was jealous of Greta—not really. But Greta was an equal to someone like Wilder Hunnicut. While Virginia herself was smart, had ambition and was halfway decent looking, she knew that being with a man like Wilder demanded a level of sophistication she did not possess.

Mrs. Hunnicut's voice cut into her thoughts. "My son dates pretty faces, but he hasn't found his heart's desire yet. When he does, he'll be loyal and loving. Just like his father," she announced proudly. "It's simply a matter of finding the right girl and he'll find happiness."

"He certainly seems happy," Virginia said.

"Well, he's not." The statement was made with conviction.

"Mrs. Hunnicut," Virginia began, folding her napkin and placing it on the table next to her plate. "I appreciate the wonderful dinner and meeting your son, seeing his home. But it's time I left. I need to get up early tomorrow. It's a workday."

"I understand. A beautiful young thing like you certainly doesn't need to hang around with an old lady who does well to play an occasional hand of bridge." She stood up and reached for her cane. "Come have a cup of tea with me, and then I'll send you on your way with Sammy."

Virginia began to protest. "I really should—"

"We still haven't discussed your reward." Mrs. Hunnicut said.

"Really, I don't need..." What in heaven's name was she saying? Of *course* she needed a reward! She needed any help she could get to take the pressure off.

Mrs. Hunnicut had already reached the dining-room door and was turning to enter the living area. "Nonsense."

There must have been a cue that Virginia hadn't seen, because Maggie came in with a pot of tea, two cups and cookies on a silver tray. She set the tray down

on the coffee table, gave a warm, conspiratorial smile
to the older woman, a shy one to Virginia, then left.

Mrs. Hunnicut poured steaming liquid into both
cups.

"I don't take anything in mine," Virginia volunteered at her hostess's silent question.

Once that ritual was over, Virginia reached for a
cookie and wished she was on her way home. A low
depression seemed to have settled over her spirits. It
came from seeing how others lived without the struggle to survive day-to-day; she envied that. *Soon*, she
promised herself. *Very soon.*

"Virginia, please open that cabinet and bring me the
oil lamp that's on the top shelf, would you?"

"Certainly," she said, going to a glass showcase. The
squat little object, made of gray and red clay, was
hardly elaborate, but line drawings painted in black
and deep red made it into a piece of art. The lamp was
small enough that it fit into the palm of her hand. She
carried it carefully back to the table and placed it next
to the silver tray. Somehow the American Indian design looked completely at home.

Mrs. Hunnicut smiled, her arthritic finger following
a black, zig-zag line. "My husband bought this land
when we were in our early twenties and struggling for
every nickel. Someone told him it would be worth
much more someday, and he believed it. I argued, but
it did no good—thank heavens. I was wrong."

Virginia glanced out the window. She could understand why Mrs. Hunnicut had had reservations. The

land gave the appearance of being wild. But it had been tamed.

"There was nothing out here then. No civilization, no housing projects, no Lake Travis. All that came later. Before Wilder built this house, we used to camp out here on the weekends, sleeping under the stars and dreaming about how we would prosper and live the rest of our days surrounded by our children, in the comfort of our family."

She sighed, then sipped her tea. Virginia remained silent. She had a feeling that her comments or questions weren't needed at this point. Mrs. Hunnicut might be an elderly lady, but she was as sharp as a tack and knew exactly where she was going. This story was definitely *not* the ramblings of an old woman.

Mrs. Hunnicut's gaze cut to the window reminiscently. "One day, while out for a hike, we walked farther down the canyon than we normally did. When we climbed to a shallow ledge, we stumbled upon a hole that led to an underground cave. That wasn't unusual for this area. What *was* different was that this cave had a small opening shielded from sight by an overgrown bush. My husband took a flashlight and went down through the hole, then disappeared. I was a nervous wreck waiting for him to return. As I recall I expected him to be chased out by a bear or some such thing." She laughed.

Virginia sat quietly, holding back her questions, knowing the story would continue.

"My husband, however, knew better. He was a geologist and loved to track animals as a hobby. He had no fear. Well, when he came out of the darkness a little while later, he held a clay lamp. It had a ropelike wick and burned animal oil—it was obviously very old. But I was more relieved to see him than I was to see the lamp." Her expression sobered, revealing the pain she felt at losing her love. "He was my life, you see. My soul mate in the true sense of the word."

"I'm so sorry," Virginia said, covering the old woman's hand with her own, knowing those words were inadequate, but were the best she could do.

"It doesn't matter," Mrs. Hunnicut assured her. "I've since learned that his spirit, ornery as it is, has remained with me. It will escort me into the next world when that time comes." Her smile was rueful. "But I didn't mean to depress you. I was telling a story. Where was I?" She frowned, then her brow cleared. "Oh, yes. Anyway, that night he cleaned up the lamp and lit it. I said something about our lack of money, and he wished he could give me a diamond big enough to make my mother sit up and take notice of him as an adequate provider. The next day he received a job offer and part ownership in a well that led to one of the largest oil strikes in this section of the country. Hard to believe, but my darling and I owned a piece of it. I had my diamond within a month of finding the lamp. Needless to say, my mother sat up and took notice of the provider my husband was. We never had to worry about money again."

"That's quite a story."

"Isn't it?" Her gray-blond bun bobbed up and down in agreement. "And there's more. According to some writings on the bottom of the lamp there are three wishes granted to whoever owns the lamp. My husband got them, I had them, and now I'm offering them to you. The only rule is that they must be possible to begin with."

"Me?" Virginia asked incredulously.

"You. I'm giving you until the end of this week to decide what you want for your reward. You may have either the lamp or five hundred dollars. Either one. But you cannot decide right away and you can't waffle or change your mind. You must make a clear-cut decision by Friday. No regrets. Understand?"

Virginia heard five hundred dollars, but the story of the lamp seemed far more real to her right this moment than the money. The lamp was the stuff that fantasies were made of, it was mystical and magical, just like tonight. Later, the reality of an unpaid phone bill would influence her choice, but for now it was fun to dream, to wish, perhaps to find reality in the wish....

Without Mrs. Hunnicut saying another word, Virginia knew she was on the horns of a dilemma.

She had four more months to struggle. Five hundred dollars would make it so much easier. But if the lamp *was* for real, the rest of her life could be certain to be a success.

Her head told her to take the money and run, but her heart said take the lamp and hold on to the hope that swelled deep in her heart.

3

ALL THE WAY HOME, the fanciful idea of a magical lamp fulfilling her every wish played Virginia's mind. Sammy, the same young man who had driven the van to Lick Creek, drove her home in a luxurious Mercedes-Benz sedan. Soft-as-a-cloud leather enveloped her. Soft music surrounded her. She only wished someone—anyone—would be here to see her arrive home, but she knew better. The street was always quiet when darkness fell. When they reached her place—an ancient house that had been broken up into apartments—she stepped out, then extended her hand to Sammy.

"Thanks," she said. "I appreciate the ride."

His youthful grin widened. "My privilege, ma'am. I'll be by to pick you up on Friday."

"Mrs. Hunnicut already told you?" she asked in surprise.

"No, but staff gossip is better than a written order from any general."

"There's a thought," Virginia stated dryly. "And I'm not sure about Friday night yet. I haven't checked my calendar to see if I'm free for the evening." Who was she kidding? The only thing that could keep her away was death on her doorstep!

"Hope you can," Sammy said. "Mrs. H. really likes you." He backed away to step into the car. "And whatever makes her happy makes the rest of us happy."

"Have a safe trip home," Virginia called as the car pulled smoothly away from the curb.

Sammy waved. The taillights disappeared when he turned the corner.

With slow steps, Virginia entered her apartment, made the coffee ready for the morning, got undressed and slipped into bed. She stared at the ceiling for all of three minutes before her eyelids drifted closed and she slept like a baby.

VIRGINIA CALLED Mrs. Hunnicut the morning after her visit and accepted her invitation to dinner on Friday, which came surprisingly fast. Virginia waited impatiently for the final hour to arrive.

She must have glanced at her watch at least a hundred times that afternoon. When she took a break, Sadie was already outside, smoking one of her customary unfiltered cigarettes. "Today's a big day, right?"

"Right." Virginia leaned back and closed her eyes, letting the afternoon sun warm her skin. "And I'm tired of it already. Since this whole episode started, it's been a war of nerves. I'm almost ready to call it off."

"Get the money first." Sadie was nothing if she wasn't practical. "You'll be glad you did when you need it next month."

"You're probably right, but it sure is wearing."

But Sadie's thoughts were elsewhere. "How'd you

like the son? Isn't he a looker? And quite the lady's man."

Virginia felt her face bloom in a high blush. Heart racing at the mere thought of Wilder, she purposely focused on other things so her expression wouldn't reveal her thoughts. She tried to act casual, as she asked, "How do you know?"

Sadie gave her a sheepish smile. "I read the gossip rags. It's an old habit. His picture is in the tabloids all the time." Her gaze skittered away, to the end of the alley. "My youngest daughter kept up with everyone who had money in this city. She was bound and determined to marry wealth and used to say that in order to marry money you had to think like money thinks."

"And did she?"

"Yes." Sadie grinned. "She married the most wealthy auto mechanic in Kerrville. They have one child, and Beverly works in the Cowboy Hall of Fame part-time. She loves her life."

"So much for marrying money." Virginia laughed.

"Hey, mechanics make good money," Sadie said defensively. "Especially if they have their own shop— and my son-in-law does. Besides, she found out that watching the wealthy was a whole lot different than hobnobbing with them."

Virginia gave a hefty sigh, reliving her own churning emotions when she'd dined with the Hunnicuts. They had been so kind and interesting, but she doubted if she could even look as self-assured and sophisticated. In Virginia's mind, they stood on a pedestal she couldn't begin to climb. Even if she was a success in her chosen field, she could never hold her own in a room full of their elevated friends.

Who was she kidding? She wasn't thinking about Mrs. Hunnicut. She loved the older woman and her outspoken ways. Virginia was totally intimidated by her *son*, however. Wilder Hunnicut was everything she wasn't: cosmopolitan, attractive as the devil, bright, successful and very, very, sexy. Intimidation made her too quick to give answers that had her sounding like an airhead, she was sure. She felt she'd said all the wrong things and gave the wrong impression. Luckily, she probably wouldn't see him again. Sammy would pick her up, take her to Mrs. Hunnicut's to collect her five-hundred-dollar reward, and then Virginia would fade out of their lives.

Both sides would be happy. Well, at least the Hunnicuts would. Virginia would forever remember wistfully her one time of hobnobbing with the wealthy.

And truth to tell, Wilder Hunnicut had left his indelible mark on her psyche. She'd probably always drool over anyone who even vaguely resembled him.

She finished her shift, then changed clothes and waited for Sammy to arrive. He was half an hour late and was driving the van.

Virginia's heart beat in double time in anticipation of dining at the Hunnicut mansion again. She wouldn't even admit to herself that she was hoping to catch just a glimpse of the man of the house. "Are we taking Mr. Hunnicut home, too?" she asked Sammy.

"Yes, but I still have to pick him up. He'll be waiting for us outside the capitol. It's been a busy day."

Her good thoughts had worked, she thought wryly. She was going to get to ride with him before he probably disappeared with Ms. Longlegs.

The capitol was only a few long blocks away, but the drive took a little over ten minutes. Traffic was usually heavy this time of day, especially when the state legislation was in session.

Virginia sat primly in the van, in a chair near the desk. It looked as if Wilder had been in the middle of a project when he'd last ridden in the vehicle. Virginia's curiosity to know what it was about was killing her, but she was afraid to disturb any of the papers scattered across the large wood-and-Formica desktop.

Sammy double-parked at the side of the regal old building that was the hub of the city. After trying the car phone without getting through, he spoke to Virginia. "I'll be right back. Mr. Hunnicut is supposed to be just inside the doors."

Virginia stared at the papers on the desk once more. Maybe he was following another stock that would be hot in the years to come. Maybe it would be the avenue to wealth and riches. Maybe...

She leaned over, tilting her head and reading a few of the charts. It *was* a stock! But which one? If she had enough reward money left after paying off her bills, maybe she could buy one more share for her portfolio. Of his stock, or perhaps another stock. One that might have a better-than-average chance of doing well because it had already been researched by an expert?

The temptation was too much. She glanced out the window quickly. Not seeing Sammy, she returned her attention to the desk, shifting the papers around to face her.

Virginia felt the flush of discovery. She was right. Some utility company in the Midwest was charted and graphed several times, the computer printouts proving its estimated growth rate. Another paper, one farther over toward the other edge of the desk, seemed to contain written material on the same stock. Or did it?

Without thinking, she reached for the sheet and plucked it from its spot in front of the computer.

A knock on the van door made her jump in her seat. She looked up, feeling her face flame as Wilder slid it open and stared at her, then at the paper in her hand. "Is it understandable or should I explain what you're reading in greater detail?"

At the first sound of Wilder's deep voice, Virginia's heart popped up into her throat, almost choking off her breath. "Oh! I—I..."

Her gaze shot to the paper as if she was shocked to find it in her hand. She reached deep inside for some semblance of composure. She wasn't an industrial spy—she was just interested in stock information.

She looked straight into his handsome face. "I'm embarrassed that you caught me, I was bored, so I started reading the graphs—they were right there, out in the open."

"And then you saw the stock report," he finished dryly. "Although it wasn't for your eyes, you decided it was fair game, too."

Virginia thought about protesting, then realized it wouldn't work. "That's about it," she said, far more calmly than she felt. "I'm sorry if I broke some kind of law. It was a bit tedious waiting...." Her voice dwindled away.

"And you're a reader." He sighed, stepping into the van and sitting in his desk chair. "You read everything in sight."

"If you'd have had computer instructions in German, I'd be sitting here trying to figure out a word or two."

He frowned. "I'm familiar with readers. My mother is one, remember?" He glared at Virginia. "So where's your book? I thought all readers carried something for occasions just like this."

"Normally, I do. But since I was carrying a small bag—" she lifted up her tiny wallet purse by its long strap "—I didn't have room for one."

"So you were bored." He held out his hand, palm up. "Do I get the report back or are you planning to keep it?"

Once more she looked down at her hand as if it belonged to someone else. Once more she blushed. "Oh. Sorry." She handed the paper to him.

"Thanks." For the first time since Wilder had appeared, he smiled. It was enough to send an electric jolt directly to her heart.

Just then, Sammy opened the front door of the van and slipped into the driver's seat. "Sorry, sir. I didn't see you leave."

Wilder's attention was distracted from Virginia, for which she was grateful. "Not a problem, Sammy. I got held up by Senator Chisom and came out the front door."

"Yes, sir."

The van pulled away smoothly from the curb and entered the flow of traffic. Virginia stared at the top of the desk, wishing for all the world that she could disappear. Where was her guardian angel—taking a vacation?

When Wilder spoke, his tone was casual. "The report is on a company that's known for its diversity. I find that interesting in an industry where most companies specialize."

Virginia gave a tentative smile in silent thanks. "I noticed it was a utility company. Do you invest in them often?"

Wilder nodded and began explaining the chart and legend. But Virginia was captivated by the way his mouth moved. His gorgeous full lips—the bottom one fuller than the top—were the sexiest things she'd ever seen. They were mesmerizing.

They? her mind scoffed. Okay, *he.* Wilder Hunnicut—all of him—was the stuff a woman's dreams were made of.

"Damn." She blushed as the word accidently slipped out.

Wilder's eyes widened. "I beg your pardon?"

It seemed that all she did around this man was blush! "Sorry, I didn't realize I was thinking out loud."

"Since we were talking about stocks, I take it you didn't like something I said."

When in doubt, tell the truth. After all, she had nothing to lose. If she spoke her mind, at least he might remember with a smile the naive, gauche woman who had thought he was terrific.

She plunged in, her voice almost breathless in the rush. "I was thinking that you are very handsome, but then you probably already know that, just by looking in the mirror. Then I thought, sure, but everyone likes to hear it, especially from someone who has no need to flatter."

"Are you trying for brownie points?"

"Of course not," she scoffed. "I'm saying it because it's true. Your mother and I have finished our business, for all intents and purposes, and there's nothing left except for me to pick up my reward—not that I believe I should receive one, but she offered and I'm accepting. Not the lamp, of course, but the cash...." Her voice trailed off as she realized that a myriad of expressions had crossed his face as she'd rattled on.

She'd done it again. She got excited and nervous, and then talked herself into a corner. "Damn," she whispered under her breath.

"Yes, I know. You think I'm handsome."

Normally, she would have laughed at that, but his

expression was so devoid of humor that she thought better of it.

She leaned back in her chair and gave a deep sigh. "I'm sorry. It's a habit I have when I'm nervous."

"Talking?"

"Babbling."

"I see," he said. "And you're nervous now."

She folded her hands in her lap and stared down at them for a minute. Then she looked him squarely in his gorgeous hazel eyes. "Yes."

"Am I making you nervous?"

"Yes." She shook her head. "No." She nodded her head. She'd done enough to make a fool of herself. It was time to stop. "Yes."

"Are you sure?"

"Yes."

"I'm sorry you feel that way." He frowned. "What lamp?"

Her eyes widened "What?"

"You mentioned a lamp." He sounded impatient. "What lamp?" It was a tone that probably worked on employees when he wanted information. But it didn't work on her.

"I believe that might be between your mother and myself, since you don't seem to know about it."

Very slowly, very calmly, he repeated himself. "What...lamp?"

Okay, so she might be a slight bit intimidated. Besides, what harm would it do to tell him? "Your mother seems to think it's a magic lamp. She said your father found it in a cave. You've never heard of it?"

Suddenly his face cleared and laughter poured, deep, thick and rich, from his throat. "My God," he finally said. "Don't tell me she's talked you into believing that story!"

"No, she hasn't." Virginia's chin tilted at a determined angle. If Wilder had been smart, he would have heeded the warning. But he didn't. "She did mention it as a choice of reward."

"And you're falling for it?" He chocked on his laughter.

"I contemplated it, just as I would any other option."

"I bet you did. I'm surprised you didn't choose it." His laughter rolled again.

That did it. Virginia sat up straight and smiled sweetly. "You know, I gave you all sorts of credit for being kind to your mother the other night. Such a successful, busy, important, good-looking man, and you took care to tease and please her. But I was wrong, wasn't I? You were secretly making fun of her all the time." Her smile disappeared. "And probably of me, too."

"Now, wait just—" he began.

But she wouldn't let him speak. "Well, I can understand that you might play the snob with me," she said in a level, deadly tone. "But not with your mother. Not unless you're just a mean-spirited man. I never would have thought it, but I guess being in the business you are and making it to the top would toughen you to your own mother, not to mention some nobody from nowhere."

"I didn't..."

"But I'm not amused by your tone." She knew her eyes sparkled with anger, but she didn't care at all. "Although I don't have to put up with it much longer. You can drop me off at your house, then go elsewhere. And later, when I'm gone, you can talk about the waif your mother picked up and duped into taking a worthless lamp because it had a weird, romantic story attached."

Her sarcasm didn't seem to faze him at all. "Well, I'll be," he said softly, his deep, rich voice filled with awe as he stared at her. He looked as if she were someone from outer space. "So you *are* going to take the lamp? God, my mother got off cheap, didn't she?"

He hadn't heard a word Virginia had said, let alone been insulted by it. "I haven't revealed what I'm going to choose, Mr. Hunnicut. I just quoted the choices your mother gave me."

He raised an all-knowing brow. "And defended them by attacking me, Ms. Gallagher."

Damn. He remembered her name. She wasn't surprised, but she did fleetingly wish he hadn't. She didn't want him mentioning her derisively in years to come. Not that he would have any reason to. After all, she wasn't stupid enough to *choose* the lamp—she was just silly enough to defend it!

The van slowed, then turned, and Virginia realized they were almost at the house. She squared her shoulders and gave him a look she saved for those she wanted to intimidate. "I'm not sure, but I just don't see this as being any of your business. This happens to be between your mother and me."

The car stopped and Sammy jumped from the front seat. In two seconds he was at the van door. Virginia was peripherally aware of all that, but her attention was focused on Wilder, who was watching her as if she were a germ under a microscope.

The door slid open. Wilder was faster than she was; he slipped from his seat, took the step down and was outside the van, watching her with a knowing look as she finally moved from her own chair.

His hand was outstretched to help her step from the van. "Allow me."

Keeping her expression as haughty as she possibly could after her last statement, she intended to be regal and graciously place her hand in his to step down. Instead, she lost her balance and fell—right into his waiting arms and against his broad chest.

Even as her breath whooshed from her lungs, she realized just how strong and thick and *hard* Wilder's chest was. Another word came to mind, but she was afraid to think about it. It was a foreign word to her, one she hadn't thought of since she was a child.

Comfort.

Virginia felt her face heat once more. "Damn," she whispered under her breath and into his chest.

"My sentiments exactly, Ms. Gallagher."

His low voice rumbled in his chest and she felt the

vibration against her cheek. It was a wonderful feeling. A wonderfully terrific feeling. A wonderfully, terrific, completely embarrassing... She pulled her head away and looked up at him.

He was staring down at her slightly parted mouth, a small smile playing on his lips.

For just a moment time seemed to stand still. She knew exactly where his hands were. One was splayed against her back while the other held her hip in a gentle but firm vise.

"Clumsy me," she said, her voice so low it sounded as if she were in a well.

"My fault," he rumbled again.

Neither moved for what seemed like an eternity. After a few, terribly long seconds, she looked up, her eyes instantly locking on those full lips she'd only seen from a distance. They were just as sexy up close.

Wilder's hands loosened, then tightened again as he gently pushed her away from his body. "Are you all right?"

"Fine. Just feeling a little stupid."

"No need. It could have happened to anyone."

"Thanks," she said. "I appreciate you sharing the blame."

"I'm not doing that," he corrected. "You fell. I was just there to catch you."

"Right." She hoped she never saw him again. Or the opposite: she wished she could see him so many times that this episode would be overlaid by all the other memories they might share.

She wished she could dissolve into the concrete at the same time his memory was wiped clean.

With careful precision, she stepped back and pulled at the hem of her sweater. The two spots where his hands had touched her skin were still hot. She had to ignore it.

"Well," she stated brightly, feeling more like an idiot than a working woman waiting for her reward for a deed well done. "I believe your mother's waiting. Shall we go?"

She walked past the two men and toward the antique front doors, telling herself that eventually there was going to be an end to this evening. All that mattered right now was that she would be five hundred dollars wealthier and two acquaintances poorer.

It just proved that life was a trade-off.

As WILDER WATCHED Virginia go into the house, he willed himself not to smile. The woman was irritating, independent, and had a big mouth full of opinions. Everything he didn't like in a female.

On the other hand, she was sweet, interested and willing to discuss any subject, and she didn't care if he knew her opinion and disagreed with it. Very unusual. Oh, and one more thing. She was soft.

When he'd held her in his arms, he'd thought how pliable she was, and how small and soft. Unusual for most skinny women. Usually they were all bones, and he hated holding a woman who felt that way.

Stop it, Hunnicut, he told himself. He was smart

enough to know that to step outside his own social circle could be dangerous. Every woman alive believed in Cinderella to some degree or another. Some more than others. It had been his experience that the poorer the woman, the greater the belief.

He didn't need that hassle.

But there was no harm in contemplating this new twist his mother had introduced. And Wilder was sure that Virginia entering the picture had been his mother's idea. He just wasn't sure why.

He'd been dating Greta off and on for over a year, but there was certainly no threat of marriage—so there was no threat that his mother would have a daughter-in-law she didn't like. In fact there was no hope of marriage to anyone.

Wilder had learned at a young age that marriage was a trade-off—and he wasn't ready to give up his freedom, money and time to have a woman in his life and heartache. Having women in his bed wasn't difficult; they saw money and came running. It didn't hurt that he was reasonably intelligent, good-looking and had a sense of humor, but their willingness made him leery all the same.

Greta was one of the few honest women he knew. She'd told him she loved his money and the wealthy society people he mixed with. She'd also told him he was good-looking and a great lover. He agreed with one and was pleased with the other—but he took both with a grain of salt. Like all women, she was capable of bending the truth to her own advantage.

Then, again, so was he. But he never lied to himself, which was why he admitted that he was attracted in an odd way to Virginia Gallagher.

After using his cell phone to cancel his plans for the evening, he followed her into the house.

He decided he wouldn't miss this meal for anything in the world. If Virginia chose the lamp, he wanted to know what her first wish would be.

4

ALL THROUGH DINNER Virginia tried to act natural, but it wasn't easy with Wilder sitting practically in front of her. Mrs. Hunnicut seemed as surprised as Virginia was by her son's presence.

Wilder was quiet most of the evening, adding very little to his mother's conversational tidbits. However, his solemn gaze was unflinching when he turned it on Virginia.

When Mrs. Hunnicut decided it was time to have coffee, she didn't bother to ask Wilder if he intended to stay. Her smile was knowing.

Wilder took the lead unexpectedly. "I understand you enjoy playing the stock market," he said. "But what else do you do? What are your dreams for the future, Ms. Gallagher?"

Virginia carefully placed her fork on her almost empty plate. Reaching for her water goblet, she looked at him warily. "As I mentioned before, I want to be a great chef someday. I'd like to have my own restaurant, where people come from all over to taste my wares."

"How often does that happen in your profession?"

His tone sounded patronizing, and she felt herself stiffen with pride.

"How often do you go to a restaurant a second or third time for the same dishes?" she asked, challenging him. "And do you order a particular entrée at only one restaurant or do you sample the same thing at others you go to?"

"Of course I compare."

"Wilder's favorite dish is a sea bass that Conrad's Restaurant makes. He swears it's never tasted the same anywhere else," his mother added brightly, totally ignoring her son's glowering look.

"Every chef goes all out for a client who loves his cooking. It's like applause to an actor."

"Have *you* ever had that happen?" Wilder asked.

"Not yet. I'm not cooking in restaurants while I'm in this last phase of my training. It's too hard to go to school and cook all day, then do the same thing at work all evening. Especially when you're not cooking what you like to cook. There's really no place that does Southwest cuisine here. Yet."

"And are you going to be the one to change that?"

Her brows rose. "Are you intimating that you doubt I could?"

His smile was delightfully crooked and slightly abashed. "I've managed to do it again, haven't I? I've stepped on your feelings."

"Yes, you have," Mrs. Hunnicut said, intervening before Virginia could open her mouth. "And you should be ashamed of yourself."

Virginia grinned. She'd never had a champion before, especially a seasoned veteran. She leaned back and watched the action.

"I was only teasing. Everyone needs a sense of humor—especially when it comes to work."

"How wise," Virginia finally said. "And how *is* the computer business?"

He played along, obviously enjoying himself. "Doing well, thank you."

"And your competition? Are they doing well, too?"

"As well as they can, considering we've got the best product out there."

"I wonder if your competition feels the same way?"

"Oh, they're worried, my dear. Why, one of those major companies tried to buy my son—"

"It's all right, Mom," Wilder said softly, his piercing, hazel gaze still riveted on Virginia. "You don't really need to defend my business."

Virginia placed her chin in the palm of her hand and leaned forward, practically batting her lashes at him. "Oh, but I'm interested."

Wilder's smile slipped. "I wouldn't want to bore you with the details."

"But you wouldn't."

Maggie came in and poured the coffee. "So," Wilder said, taking a sip from his cup. "What's next? Is this when you ask Virginia to actually make her choice?"

Mrs. Hunnicut's eyes widened. "My, aren't we forward!" she exclaimed, her gaze darting between her son and Virginia. "Is that why you decided to stay home for dinner, Wilder? You thought there was going to be a floor show?"

His grin was tolerant. "Not at all. But I didn't want to miss a thing." He leaned back and trained his eyes on Virginia once more. "The thought of Ms. Gallagher's selection is intriguing. I was sure she would choose the lamp, but she disabused me of that notion very quickly."

"That wasn't what I said at all, Mr. Hunnicut. If you're referring to our discussion on the drive here, then please be accurate."

"Sorry. I must have forgotten. It doesn't happen often, but occasionally I forget a thing or two. Would you like to refresh my memory?"

"Are they pickin' on you, Mr. Hunnicut?" Maggie asked. She was carrying three plates of steaming-hot apple cobbler drizzled with cream.

"Something terrible, Maggie. I think Ms. Gallagher might be a latent male-basher."

"Bosh," Mrs. Hunnicut stated firmly. But Virginia spotted a definite gleam in her eye. "For some reason you've been baiting this lovely lady all night. I think you owe her an apology."

Wilder gave a bowing nod that looked more regal than deferential. "I'm sorry for any wrongdoing, Ms. Gallagher. I meant no offense. And I forgive you for anything *you* might have said or done that was amiss."

"Really, Wilder..." his mother began.

"Accepted, and no offense taken, Mr. Hunnicut," Virginia retorted, giving the same regal nod. Damn his soul. He was referring to her looking through his papers.

"Wilder," his mother repeated.

"And just what are you going to choose?" he asked, catching Virginia off guard. She hadn't expected that subject to come up until after he'd left and she was alone with his mother. She'd thought she'd made herself clear on that point.

But, just in case he didn't understand, she made it clear again. "That is between your mother and me." She didn't want to see his knowing look when she chose the money.

"I think it would be lovely if Wilder heard your choice," his mother said. "Especially if it's what I think it is. It's about time he realized that not all people make decisions based on financial advantage alone."

Wilder's grin broadened, his eyes danced. Although he spoke to his mother, his gaze was focused on Virginia. "Somehow, Mom, I think you're in for a rude awakening."

"You don't know that, dear. Virginia is Irish, you know. She understands the fey and mystical qualities of life and happenings. She's not just another beautiful woman waiting to drape herself on some good-looking man so she has an identity. She's *with it, out there.* She's doing something that changes her life, not waiting for others to do it for her." The older woman sniffed disdainfully.

Virginia wished she didn't like the compliments. It made her feel obligated....

"All that and more," Wilder murmured.

Virginia couldn't meet his gaze anymore. She stared down at the napkin in her lap and wished she'd never found the wallet. Now she was going to be either a money grubber or fey and a leader of together women, a hip but poor go-getter.

"What *is* your decision, my dear?" Mrs. Hunnicut asked softly. "Please don't allow us to pressure you one way or the other. The decision is truly up to you."

Virginia looked thankfully at the older woman, grateful she'd said that. But they both knew Mrs. Hunnicut was rooting for the lamp.

Virginia glanced at Wilder and wished she hadn't done so. The knowing look on his face put iron in her spine. Even as she turned again to his mother, Virginia wished she wasn't going to do what she had to....

"I need the money, Mrs. Hunnicut—there's not a doubt in my mind about that. But I also believe you're right. Sometimes things have to be taken on faith." She took a deep breath, hoping the right words would come out. "I'd like to have the lamp, please."

Her heart sank at her own spoken words.

Wilder looked as stunned as she felt.

Mrs. Hunnicut looked positively smug. "And so you shall, my dear. And you'll see. All those other pesky little problems will disappear if you make the proper wishes."

"I hope so. I sincerely hope so," Virginia said fervently.

"Well, I'll be damned." Wilder's comment was so low it was barely a whisper. "I don't believe it."

It sounded like thunder to her ears. Virginia could hardly believe it, either. She wanted to cry, both in relief and in disappointment. At least the decision was over. So were her hopes for paying off the phone company.

VIRGINIA RECEIVED strict orders on how to make the lamp work. Mrs. Hunnicut was very explicit and very, very kind. It was as if she took pity on inadvertently duping Virginia out of her five-hundred-dollar reward.

Wilder didn't follow them into the living room. In fact, he didn't show up again until Virginia was ready to leave.

As if by magic, he was suddenly standing in the doorway, his hands in his sweat-suit pockets. "I'm driving Virginia back, Mom. I gave Sammy the night off." Virginia wondered if he'd been listening outside the room, but realized that it didn't really matter. Once she was home, she was going to cry herself to sleep. Then she would wake up in the morning and realize she had had a wonderful adventure and it was over. After all, it wasn't as if she'd lost something. She wasn't any further behind, she just wasn't any further ahead.

Mrs. Hunnicut gave her shoulders a squeeze. "Good luck, my dear. I know you'll be successful at whatever you do, including choosing your wishes carefully. Remember, think about the way you word them so you get the most from each wish."

Virginia smiled wanly. "Thank you. I will." More hopes would probably be dashed to bits over this.

Wilder helped her into the front seat of the Mercedes sedan and drove to the highway. After Virginia gave directions to her house, she sat back for the ride. They hit the highway, and silence reigned.

Wilder's strong profile was illuminated by the dashboard lights. His nose was straight and noble, there was an indentation just above those full lips, his strong chin had a slight cleft and his high cheekbone could have been carved from marble. He was the epitome of masculinity. Virginia had seen men more handsome, but never more masculine. He could have been a movie star, yet it wasn't hard to imagine him leading a board meeting or commanding front-line forces in some military action. He had the aura of a leader.

Obviously she wasn't alone in her estimation of Wilder Hunnicut, she thought wryly. He was head of one of the most powerful computer corporations in the U.S., one that was growing stronger every day.

"Computer chip for your thoughts."

His words snapped her back to the present. "I was just thinking that you have a certain aura that allows others to think you'll lead them in the right direction, and they probably follow like sheep."

"Everyone but you."

"Except me."

"I think I knew that at the dinner table tonight." He

glanced at her, his expression puzzled. "So tell me. What was it that made you change your mind and choose the lamp?"

"What do you mean?" she hedged.

"I mean that you were going for the money right up to the end. What changed your mind in a split second?"

She thought about defending her position, but her heart wasn't in it. She was holding a box containing a clay pot with a wick instead of a purse holding buffer money for the next four months. He might as well share the blame. "You did."

"Me?"

"You. You goaded me into thwarting your guess. As if you didn't know."

He ignored her last comment. "My, my, I thought you were more...determined than to allow a stranger to dissuade you."

"Normally that would be the case," she conceded. "But I was already torn between the two decisions and when you made fun of your mother's choice of rewards, well..."

"You should have stuck to your guns."

"Like you did when it was offered to you?"

"It was never offered to me. My parents knew how I felt about such nonsense. For a while Mom was holding out, waiting to give it to my bride. But now that she knows there's not going to be one for a very long time, she's given up on that idea."

Virginia wanted to pursue that subject, but didn't have enough nerve. "Lucky you."

He grinned. "Besides, the cryptic scrawl on the wall where it was found said only two sets of wishes per family. As it was, Mom made the last wish for Dad."

"And did it come out okay?"

"If you want to call it that."

Her curiosity was fired. Mrs. Hunnicut hadn't said a word about this. "What was her wish?"

"She wished that Dad wouldn't die of a heart attack. He was in the hospital at the time, after a massive coronary. They told Mom he wouldn't survive the next one."

"So her wish came true?"

"Right," Wilder stated dryly. "He died of an aneurism, instead."

"While he was in the hospital?"

"No," he admitted grudgingly. "Five years later."

"So for all you know, it might have prolonged his life for five years. He got to spend that much more time with your mom. Sounds like a good wish to me."

"If you believe in the power of that lamp, I guess you can believe anything. Anyway, it doesn't matter. Dad believed in it long enough to recuperate and enjoy life some. For that reason, I'll thank the damn lamp."

Wilder pulled up in front of the old house she called home. Instead of ending the conversation, he turned the engine off and sat sideways, crooking his knee in the seat so he could face her.

The fact that he wasn't racing away gave her the

nerve to continue the conversation. "But you tried to persuade me against choosing it. Why?"

"I just didn't want you to get burned, pardon the pun. I knew my mother liked you very much if she was offering you the lamp. She's wanted to pass it along for a long time, but never found anyone 'worthy,' as she says. I'm surprised she found you at all."

"Not that I'd want to be in the running, but did you say you weren't interested in marriage? I thought most men wanted to propagate the earth."

Wilder shrugged. "Women have a habit of demanding more than I can give. I'm not leaving my business to baby-sit some woman who should be able to take care of herself. I've worked too hard. As long as I'm single, I can call the shots."

"I see," she said thoughtfully, cocking her head. "A control freak."

"I come by it honestly," he admitted. Seemingly without realizing it, he stroked the top of her shoulder with his thumb, slowly and seductively. "My mother is into control, in case you haven't noticed. She's behind this whole thing, if you ask me."

Virginia tried to concentrate on his words instead of his intimate touch. "Are you saying you think my finding the wallet was a setup?"

He gave a smile. "So it crossed your mind, too?"

She nodded. "It did, but I don't see how it could have happened."

"I don't, either, but my mother is a very smart woman. She would have figured out a way." He stared into Virginia's eyes. "Do you remember ever seeing her before?"

That was an easy answer. "Never."

The car was silent. Virginia could hear her own heart beating rapidly. She was expecting...waiting...for what? Her tension grew.

Just as she decided it was time to reach for the door handle and say good-night, Wilder did something that stopped her cold.

He took his hand from her shoulder and traced the side of her cheek, her chin. "You're really very lovely," he said.

"It just took you awhile to be bowled over. Right?"

His smile melted her heart. "Right. Yours is a subtle beauty, Virginia. One that sneaks up and wows a man before he knows it."

In the dark it was easier to admit to thoughts and frailties. "I think I'd rather have that full-blown beauty. The kind that slaps you in the face." Her tone was dry. So was her throat.

He continued his sensual foray, tracing the outline of her parted lips. "Beautiful mouth."

"Thank you. My mother would be pleased. She used to say she designed it."

They could have been on a desert island, and Virginia would have felt the same way. There was only one other person in the world, and he was sitting next to her. Her breath was shallow and her pulse fluttered so quickly it would barely register.

"You're really very beautiful," he said softly. His

voice was a husky whisper that warmed every part of her.

"Thank you. You're very handsome." The least she could do was return the compliment, especially when it was true.

She could tell he was trying to keep from smiling. "Thank you." His thumb pressed lightly on her chin, and her mouth parted in response. "May I kiss you?"

Honesty was always the best policy. "Yes." Her voice was just a thread of sound.

Wilder leaned forward and so did Virginia. Slowly, ever so slowly, he pressed his lips on hers. The contact was electrifying and perfect. A tiny breath escaped her and he captured it with his lips.

It was a kiss like no other she'd ever experienced. From the moment his lips touched hers, she began floating on a cloud of high emotion. She reached out, holding on to his shoulders as the ride became frightening. It was as if she'd lost her balance or was soaring through the skies without a parachute. Wilder was all there was between her and the ground.

He pulled her closer, then into his lap as the kiss deepened. His tongue danced in her mouth, daring her to answer his silent message thrusting in imitation of lovemaking.

Wilder held her head in his hands, tilting her mouth so he could have better access. She complied, allowing him to do anything as long as she was a part of it.

Her hands tightened slightly, possessively, kneading his shoulders, seeking a path down his neck and back, seeking and feeling the rock-hard muscle of him. Loving what she felt.

There was a low moan and it took a hazy moment to realize it came from Wilder, not her. When he began pulling away, she was reluctant to let him go.

He took a deep breath and rested his moist forehead on hers. "I'm sorry, I didn't expect that," he finally admitted, his voice rough and gravelly. The sound made her tingle.

Virginia gave a nervous chuckle. "Neither did I."

Wilder dropped his hands to her waist. With the strength she now knew he was capable of, he lifted her, sitting her back on the passenger seat. "Sorry. I didn't mean... I wasn't trying..."

She pushed her hair back from her face and, taking a deep breath, told a lie. "No harm done, no offense taken."

"I'm sorry." His tone was short, curt and to the point. Obviously he didn't want to do *that* again.

"So am I." She felt cold without his body heat. Her heart was heavy with embarrassment.

He gave a lopsided grin. "It was certainly, uh, different, meeting you, Ms. Gallagher. Very refreshing."

"Thank you. You're not exactly the man on the street yourself," she responded, attempting to retain her dignity as she scrambled for her purse. It had dropped to the floorboard somewhere and the car was so dark she only had her sense of touch to rely on. "And I appreciate your mother's gift. Don't feel too bad about my choice. I *did* choose it by myself, so I have no one to blame for that."

His laughter filled the car. "You could have had the upper hand, you know. If you'd kept quiet, I might have felt guilty for the rest of my life. Or maybe I'd have written you a check for five hundred just to appease my conscience."

"Well, you can still do that. I'm game to oblige if it will help a friend in need."

"Who's the friend? You or me?"

"Both."

"But you've *already* made me feel better."

"Oh, well, my loss. Again." She reached for the door handle. "Thank you for the ride home. I appreciate it. It was a pleasure meeting both you and your mother, Mr. Hunnicut."

His smile still lighting his eyes, he offered her his hand. "The pleasure was all mine, Virginia. Have a great life."

She shook his hand once, curtly, then stepped out, slamming the door before running toward the dilapidated old house.

It was a beautiful night, but her insides felt as if they were alternating between freezing and a hundred degrees. Virginia never looked back. She went straight to her apartment and unlocked the door. Before she could get inside, she heard him drive off.

"A million to one he's not heading home," Virginia muttered. He was probably on his way to some chic party where the women were more savvy and blatantly beautiful than she could ever hope to be. They also probably held in their less-than-middle-of-the-road opinions and didn't give as many honest answers. *Those* people had tact.

"Go ahead, Gallagher," she told herself. "Stomp on your hard-won self-image." But she was a survivor, she couldn't stomp on that. *They* didn't need to scratch around to survive. *They* weren't worried about the cost of a tank of gas or having one good piece of meat a week. *They* were worried about whether or not their stockings were sheer enough or if they'd read the latest bestseller and formed the right opinion about it.

The more Virginia talked to herself, the more depressed she became. But she couldn't seem to stop the litany of differences between her and *them*.

She finally sat down and cried, thinking, *To heck with being the big, strong woman.*

MUCH LATER THAT NIGHT Virginia crawled out of bed and sat on the living-room floor, using her old couch as a backrest. Moonlight poured through her window, casting the pattern of the windowpanes on the old rug. She was caught up in the moment. Her mind had been spinning all night. No sense worrying about not choosing the money. She still had the lamp, and it wouldn't cost a thing to go through the process and see if it worked.

She thought and thought of what she wanted her first wish to be. Then, carefully filling and lighting the small clay pot, she began the process Mrs. Hunnicut had described to her. She turned the bowl around and around, watching the small yellow flame dance.

"I wish I had a job that would give me enough money to live comfortably and still have time to pay attention to the last four months of my studies, so that I'll be a success in my chosen field," she murmured into the dark. Then she added, just in case the gods weren't finicky about the one-sentence law that Mrs. Hunnicut had spoken about, "And if Wilder Hunnicut was occasionally available to be reminded of my success in that role—whatever it was—then it would be all the better."

She sat back with a sigh.

There, she'd done it.

Maybe it was no more than a stupid game, but she'd followed through and stated her first wish. It was the consolation prize for not choosing the money. If Wilder hadn't goaded her, she'd be sitting here writing a check to the phone company, instead of talking to a lamp.

That wasn't quite true, she admitted. She'd *allowed* herself to be goaded by the man. It had been her choice right up until she uttered the words. No fair burdening him with more blame than he deserved, especially when she could kick her *own* butt so well.

Just as the dark night sky began to lighten, Virginia crawled into bed. She had two more hours before she had to be in class, and she meant to take advantage of every minute.

WILDER STOOD ON THE DECK of his home, wrapped in a warm bathrobe, and stared at the dim light growing in the east. Dawn was breaking and he hadn't had more than a few hours sleep. Again. He shivered.

At least this time he couldn't blame parties or the stress at work. No. This time he had something else to blame. Or some*one* else. Virginia Gallagher. She was a smart lady who hid her brains under soft, strawberry blond hair. With her discerning blue eyes, she saw more than most people did. By her slim figure he knew she might be the world's best chef, but she didn't eat with any regularity. She was taller than the average woman, perhaps five seven or eight, but she didn't slouch or try to pretend she was petite. And she was proud. She always looked him in the eye.

She'd been invading his thoughts since he'd met her. But now, ever since he'd canceled a party in order to drop her off at that ill-constructed lumber heap called a house, he knew he was fascinated. The kiss—more heady and sexually stimulating than any kiss he'd ever experienced—had really screwed him up.

No, that wasn't quite true. He'd been attracted to her from the start, but he'd tried to shy away by being obstinate, occasionally rude, sometimes patronizing. A total bore.

He'd never tried to goad a woman before. This was a first. Why had he goaded Virginia into taking that worthless lamp? He'd known what he was doing at the time, but he couldn't seem to let go. It didn't make any sense, but that woman brought out something foreign in him. It was something he hadn't tamed or controlled before because he'd never felt it.

She made him feel frustrated, irritated, surprised, and he enjoyed it. With her, nothing was predictable. He hoped, for her sake, of course, that things went well for her. She needed a boost to keep her going until she got through chef's school, but he had a feeling some help would turn up. She was quick, bright, resourceful and certainly capable. She'd gotten along with his mother, so he knew she'd be okay. His mother was the ultimate survivor.

A narrow window of sky grew light. It looked like a candle flame far in the distance. He blinked his eyes, then it was gone.

Interesting.

Seconds later, an idea came to him and he knew what he was going to do.

In the doing, it just might help Virginia, his mother and his own living, breathing conscience.

"And I thought it was dead," he muttered to no one in particular. But the itch in his gut eased as he thought of the action he would take after talking to his mother and convincing her it was a workable plan.

It would be a win-win-win scenario, his favorite kind....

5

IT HAD BEEN A THOROUGHLY rotten day. No sooner had Virginia paid the telephone bill than the electricity was cut off. She'd paid the bill just before coming to work, and hoped the lights would be back on when she reached home. To top it all off, business was slow and tips were down. In the lull, Tally had her cleaning out the storage closet—something Virginia didn't even do at home if she could help it. Sadie said all of congress was ordering takeout and working at their desks. Great.

Virginia was picking up tables, loading her tray, when Sadie bumped her with a hip. "*Psst.* Look who's at the window table," she whispered.

"Who?"

"Your guy."

"I don't have a..." Virginia's body went liquid with one of those hot flashes Sadie was always talking about. She whipped her head around. "Where?"

"Table 14."

Wilder Hunnicut sat with a cup of coffee in front of him, reading a newspaper, looking as handsome as ever. His head was bowed, his strong shoulders moved and she knew the feel of those muscles rippling under the cloth. He pursed his lips and she knew the taste of them.

She had another hot flash before she put some backbone in the place where her spine should have been. Of course, she'd seen him just four days ago, when he'd dropped her off at her door. They'd completed their business then. What the heck was he doing here now? If he expected to get his mother's lamp back, he was very sadly mistaken. Virginia had grown attached to the small lamp sitting on her bedside table. It held a place of honor.

She set her tray on the kitchen counter and marched up to table 14 almost defiantly, though she wasn't sure what she was defending. "May I help you?"

She pretended not to melt when he gave her that slow, easy smile. "You're looking good, Virginia. How are you?"

"Healthy, wealthy and wise, thank you."

"How's the lamp?"

"Why?" She narrowed her gaze. "You want to buy it back?"

He chuckled, a deep, warm rumble. "No. At least not today. Actually, I was wondering if I could interest you in a proposition."

Virginia leaned her hip against the table. "Okay. Shoot."

"Just like that? Aren't you going to take offense at the word *proposition?*"

She grinned unrepentantly. "Not until I hear what you're proposing."

He chuckled again. "Fair enough. Can you type?"

"Yes."

"Can you file?"

Now she was puzzled. "Yes. I learned my alphabet at a young age. What's up?"

"My mother is looking for a part-time social secretary, and I could use some help in that area, too. It comes with a salary, room and board and all expenses paid. Are you interested?"

Virginia's knees weakened. "Are you kidding?"

His sexy smile was indulgent. "This is on the level. I promise."

"How much is part-time? I have to go to school."

He brushed her problems aside. "We know and we can work around that. The main thing is that you'd be there in the early morning and evening to send out invitations or organize reminders, appointments and driving schedules for the next day. That will take a load off my mother's mind. She gets worried when things aren't organized the way she wants them."

Excitement built inside Virginia, but she was still afraid to let it show. It was almost too good to be true. Almost? Did she think almost? It *was* too good to be true! "When does it start? How much money?"

"Tomorrow." He named a salary that opened her eyes wide.

She tried to catch her breath. It wasn't easy. "I need to give a week's notice here."

Wilder shrugged. "Whatever. I need you in the house by the end of the week at the latest." He pulled out a business card and wrote a number on the back. "Natalie is my administrative assistant. Call her and she'll make all the arrangements."

"For moving?"

"For everything." He put away his pen and leaned back, looking relaxed and at ease. "You'll like Natalie. She's a take-charge kind of person. If you need to store your furniture, she can handle that, too. She'll also brief you on a few of the upcoming engagements that Mom will need help with." He stood and Virginia had to take a step back or lose the air around her. She stared up, her heart fluttering in her breast at the mere closeness of him. Instantly, she was back in his arms in the darkness of the car, kissing him with an abandon she hadn't known she was capable of.

The same thought must have flitted through Wilder's mind; she could see it in his hazel eyes. They flashed, then slowly grew calm. He purposely looked away. Tossing down a five-dollar bill he said, "The day you move in is the day your pay begins."

Virginia stared at his profile, then down at the card. "I'll only be able to work for four months."

Wilder placed his hand on her shoulder and gave a light squeeze. The squeeze turned into a stroke. Then, as if he realized what he was doing, he dropped his hand. "I know. It's okay."

He tucked the newspaper under his arm. From the look on his face, she guessed he was tickled to find her so stunned. She wished she could look calm and collected, but it was impossible. She couldn't even think!

Wilder walked out the door and Virginia watched him step into the van, which pulled away from the curb almost immediately. His offer rang in her ears. She couldn't believe it. A job from heaven. A job where she didn't have to worry about a roof over her head or food on the table.

Sadie walked up. "Well? What did the handsome Mr. Hunnicut want? Your body or your cooking?"

"Neither. He wants me to help his mother." Virginia looked at her friend. "He's giving me room and board and a great salary, plus I'll still be able to go to school." Her good fortune suddenly hit her full force and she gave in to the happiness building inside her. "Oh, Sadie! Isn't it wonderful?" she exclaimed, giving the woman a hug.

"I take it you're giving notice?" the older woman stated dryly, but there was a mistiness in her eyes that told the real story. "I'm happy for you, honey." She gave Virginia a kiss on the cheek as well as an answering hug. "Just be careful."

"Why? It sounds perfect to me."

"Too perfect." Sadie gave her a hard look. "Mark my words. That man wants your body."

Virginia felt a tinge of heat on her cheeks and laughed it off. "Mark *my* words, Sadie. He wouldn't have to do much talking to get it."

"You really like him?"

"Like" was an understatement. "Yes."

"Then go for it, girl." Sadie said. "When is your last day?"

"When can you let me go?"

"Day after tomorrow."

"I'll be gone then." She gave her friend another hug. "But I'll be back to see you, Sadie. You can't get off the hook that easily."

Sadie gave her a wrinkled grin. "You'd better." She turned and glanced at the counter, where heat lights guarded the newly cooked food. "Now, get that order to the table before they ask for a free meal."

Virginia floated over and did what she was told. In fact she floated for the rest of the day, until it was time to float home....

AFTER SHE CALLED NATALIE the next day, everything speeded up. Movers came in and took over packing all her stuff. And her old furniture was delivered to a battered-woman's shelter. In less than four days from the time Wilder had made his offer, she was relocated.

Her head spun from everything being accomplished so quickly.

ONE DAY she watched her furniture being carted away, and the next she woke up in a spacious bedroom perched on the side of a cliff overlooking Lick Creek. She sipped coffee from her own small coffeemaker as she stood at the railing of her very own private deck that hung out over the rushing water below. She watched a hawk dip and sway on the air currents above and took a deep breath of the fresh, hill-country air.

It was a fairy tale come true. If she was dreaming, she didn't want to waken.

She'd risen early to enjoy the beginning of a new day and had been on the balcony for over an hour. She was due at school in two hours. Today's challenge was canapés, and she'd worked hard at creating her own special version of an egg roll, Southwest style. It was time to get moving. With great reluctance, she left the view and began getting ready for the other changes in her life.

FROM THE SIDE PATIO, Wilder watched the rusty yellow Volkswagen pull out of the drive. He could see Virginia's strawberry blonde hair from here.

"Is that racket her car?" Mrs. Hunnicut asked. She was sitting at the wrought-iron table on the patio, enjoying her last cup of coffee for the day.

"Yes." He grinned. "Have you forgotten what it was like to be poor, Mom? You have to make do with what you can afford."

"No, I didn't forget. But that doesn't mean I like the noise. Why don't you have Manuel look at the engine and see if there's anything he can do?"

"I will," Wilder said, then paused thoughtfully. "Do you think this will work out?"

"Of course it will," his mother stated firmly. "Virginia came down this morning, had a glass of juice, practically kissed my cheek in gratitude. Then she spent an hour straightening out my schedule before she headed out the door. She's pretty, bright, caring and loving. I couldn't ask for more in a part-time secretary. She's everything I'd heard she was...."

"And just when did you hear this, Mom?" Wilder asked softly, turning to confront his mother. He'd known this was a setup—a way for his mother to introduce him to yet another woman who would make a wonderful daughter-in-law. It had helped him keep his distance with Virginia until that night in the car. He'd been so adamantly against being set up and pressured into marriage that his mother had obviously found another way to matchmake.

"When I checked her references, dear," she stated innocently. "She has a friend named Sadie who couldn't say enough kind things about her. And Sadie just happens to use the same bookstore I do. We met there—by accident, of course."

"Of course," he echoed, still smelling a fish but unable to locate it.

"Sadie's known Virginia for quite a while," his mother continued. "She said how reliable and smart she was. And the owner of the bookstore said she's been a regular customer there for the past year and reads everything she can get her hands on." She looked out at the garden, then back at Wilder. "I trust a reader, dear. Don't you?"

"Of course," he said dryly. "I don't have any choice. They're everywhere." He had to give his mother credit. She'd covered her tracks well. But sooner or later, he'd find out her game, and then he'd stop it. Until then, he'd play along....

"You always have a choice, son," his mother admonished. "You're just smart enough to know when I'm right."

"Talk to you tonight," he said, giving her a kiss on the cheek. "I've got to run."

"Have a good day, dear. I'll see you then." She watched Wilder walk away before throwing out the last question. "Will you be home for dinner tonight?"

"Not tonight. I've got a meeting with marketing," he called before turning the corner. Sammy was waiting next to the van, ready to whisk him back to the real world. He'd worry about Virginia later.

"I certainly hope you get to eat at home a little more now that we both have some help."

He pretended he didn't hear her. Hiring Virginia had been his idea, but his mother acted as if it was hers. And now she would ask for more of his attention to boot. It was up to him to make sure she didn't tread on his need for solitude.

A little voice mocked his thoughts. Anything his mother set her heart on, she got. She'd always worked toward getting whatever she wanted until she'd worn down his father and himself. Wilder had a feeling he was going to see that determined streak again. Maybe he should have put her on his board of directors.

It was all his fault, of course. By hiring Virginia, he'd planted the apple tree right in the middle of his Garden of Eden. "Damn," he muttered as the van headed toward Austin.

But there was still a ghost of a smile on his lips at the

thought of the good-looking but crazy girl in the beat-up Volkswagen.

"AND TOMORROW YOU HAVE a two-thirty appointment with your opthomoligist for your annual exam," Virginia stated, checking her new appointment calendar.

"I'll need Sammy for that, dear," Mrs. Hunnicut said, sipping her tea. She sat in a rocking chair by the open French doors. It was a warm, sunny day and light breezes scooted around the room. "Would you tell him so he knows? Oh, and tomorrow morning I promised myself I'd go to the bookstore, too. I'll need Sammy an hour earlier, so I can do both while I'm out."

"Of course." Virginia scribbled down the information, then peered at the rest of her notes. Good, she'd covered everything. "And Mr. Hunnicut said he'd be home for dinner tonight and would you ask Maggie to make a salad for him."

"She won't be home tonight, dear. I told her to make a sandwich for me and leave early." The older woman looked worried. "I wish Wilder would make up his mind whether or not he wants to dine at home. He just needs to settle down to a regular schedule," she complained.

"He leads a busy life." Virginia said quietly, not wanting to admit that she would love to see more of him, too. Her thoughts seemed to be wrapped around him from the time she awoke to the time her head hit the pillow. She wished it wasn't that way, but after living here for the past week, she'd resigned herself to it.

"He's a political animal with a brilliant mind," his mother said proudly. "Still, he needs to settle down and begin a family. It will give him a different focus. A better one. It did wonders for his father."

Virginia couldn't see Wilder settling down. Actually, that wasn't true. She didn't *want* to see him settling down. If he did, chances were it would be with some society bombshell, and that would break her heart....

"Don't worry about dinner. I'll make a salad for all of us." She looked at the older woman. "That is, if you don't think Maggie will mind my working in her kitchen."

"She won't mind a bit, dear, as long as everything goes back the way it was. It's been done before, you know." Her eyes twinkled. "And what kind of salad will it be?"

Virginia laughed. "Just an ordinary salad. After all, it's someone else's kitchen. I'll have to use whatever's available."

"If I know Maggie, you'll have everything you could possibly want. Wilder is notorious for coming home late and asking for a salad. You might get together with her, though, and discuss it."

"I will," Virginia promised. "Is there anything else you can think of that I might have missed?"

"Nothing, dear. Natalie is such an extraordinary girl. She manages all of our lives and still maintains her dignity—even while she's telling some of those stuffed shirts on the board how the cow ate the cabbage. She's kept all of us straight. She took on the duty when his secretary couldn't handle it anymore. But as Wilder's assistant, her day begins before you and I even dream of waking, and she does far too much. Wilder is worried that she'll burn out and leave him, so anything that lessens her burden is a blessing as far as he's concerned."

Virginia felt a little envious of Natalie. When they'd met, Virginia had been impressed by her professional attitude. She seemed to know everything and be on top and in control of it. At the same time, she had a disposition that was sunny and funny—carefree. But the main reason Virginia was envious was that Wilder and Natalie were on the same wavelength, living in the same world. She was amazed that they didn't date.

She stood up, notes in hand. "I'll check with Natalie later this afternoon and make sure we're all caught up with your schedule," she said. "And I'll see you this evening."

"Thank you, dear." Mrs. Hunnicut's mind was obviously elsewhere. She held a small tapestry in her lap and was studying it with intense concentration.

Ten minutes later, the phone rang and Virginia picked it up to find Wilder on the other end.

"How's it going?" he asked.

She delighted in hearing his voice. "I won't tell my employer it's a piece of cake. Instead, I'll say details, details, details. So much to remember and so little room for error. I just don't know if I can keep track of it all—even with this super-duper carrying calendar."

"Don't bother trying to tell me it's a piece of cake, because your employer wouldn't believe you, anyway. Natalie said you're the first woman who's as quick and savvy as she is. And she means it. She doesn't give out compliments often."

"And you believe her?"

"Of course." Wilder laughed. "That's why she's my assistant."

Virginia said the first thing that came to her mind. "That doesn't say much for your regular secretary."

His laughter continued. "See what I mean? Quick. So don't hand me any grief by denying the obvious. Besides, my secretary is more a liaison between the corporation and myself—she handles all the details of business. Natalie is my personal assistant, which means she works apart from my secretary but in conjunction with her. See?"

"No, but I'm sure you understand it all."

"Of course," he answered smoothly. "Which brings me to the reason I called. I left a file at home and I need it. Can you bring it to me on your way to school?"

"I don't have school today, but of course I can bring you the file. Where is it and where do I bring it?"

Wilder answered both questions and Virginia hung up, happiness flooding her. His compliment on her intelligence warmed her very heart. It wasn't the first time someone had said she was smart but it had always been in a different context before, as in "You're so bright, why don't you *do* something with yourself?" or "You're too bright not to stay in school and make something of yourself." Then, of course, there was

"You're too bright for me. Didn't anyone ever tell you that men don't like to be upstaged?"

This was the first time such a remark had made her feel proud of herself. Strange how a few words of the right kind of encouragement could change one's outlook on the world.

She checked her makeup, what little she wore, and picked up the file from Wilder's office.

After notifying Sammy of Mrs. Hunnicut's schedule she drove her car toward Austin, singing a sad country song at the top of her lungs and feeling for all the world like the happiest person alive.

Go figure, as Sadie used to say.

The entrance to Wilder's corporate headquarters was daunting. In fact, there seemed to be several entrances. She followed the written directions and found an empty parking space next to Wilder's, as he'd said she would.

Five minutes later she was laughing with Natalie as the younger woman related a story about a client wandering around the complex, lost for over two hours. When they found him, he was begging to go back home.

"Why didn't he call as soon as he realized how large the complex was and that he was lost?"

"I don't know, but I suspect it was a matter of pride," Natalie said, disgust lacing her voice. "He was a macho type and wouldn't ask directions from anyone. Probably thought he was a terrific tracker in another life. But by the time I found him, he admitted that he would have left a long time ago if he could have found his car. He'd lost that, too."

Wilder stepped out of his office carrying a handful of papers. His jacket was off and his crisp white shirt and red-and-blue tie gave him a powerhouse look. "Well, good morning, Ms. Gallagher. Glad you made it."

"Good morning, boss. Nothing to it when you know how to do it," she quipped. "You look like you're in the midst of a project."

"I am." He glanced at Natalie and gave a quick smile. "Although there are some of us who seem to be able to skim along without working up a sweat."

Natalie didn't return his smile. "That's me. Ask a woman to do a job and she gets it done right. Ask a man and he gets all hot and bothered."

"I'm getting out of here. Two women with big mouths is a little hard to handle. I might plead harassment."

"You might, Mr. Hunnicut," Natalie said, as if considering his chances. "But you wouldn't win."

"Thanks."

He looked so forlorn that both women laughed. But when another man walked up, Wilder was back to business and so was Natalie. It was as if they'd both donned professional masks, having let down their guard only when no one could see them. No one but Virginia. She felt privileged.

"Allan. Can you step into my office a moment? I need to discuss something with you," Wilder said, leading the now-nervous man into his office.

"I forgot to give him his file," Virginia said, her voice hushed even though the door was closed.

Natalie turned toward the desk where the secretary usually sat and reached for her own phone-message slips. "Don't worry. He asked that you stay for a few minutes. You're next on the rug."

"Oh, goody," Virginia said, trying to be flippant so Natalie wouldn't know how excited she was by seeing Wilder again. "I get to be yelled at, too."

"Wilder never yells. He gets quiet, and you can see the barely leashed storm brewing, but he never lets it go." Natalie smiled. "I can see where he's going before he gets there. He reminds me of someone else I know."

Virginia was curious. "Anyone I know?"

"No. He's the man I'm going to marry. He doesn't know it yet, though." The look of determination on her face said more than her words.

Virginia smiled. Poor man didn't know when to fight and when to give in. She bet Natalie would be a formidable enemy if she chose to be. "He doesn't stand a chance if what Wilder—Mr. Hunnicut—and his mother say about you is true."

Just then the door to Wilder's office opened and both men stepped out. "I'll get back to you on that," Allan promised, stepping out of the room before smiling over his shoulder and hurrying down the hall. It was obvious he was relieved to be out of there.

Wilder raised one eyebrow. "Virginia? Would you come in here, please?"

"His master's voice," she said under her breath.

Natalie grinned. "Only in a manner of speaking," she whispered back. "Hang in there. It might be pleasant."

Wilder's office was large and beautifully decorated, with contemporary lines and bright colors blended with soft whites. At one end was a broad, limestone desk and at the other was a matching conference table and twelve chairs. Virginia found it all very impressive.

He leaned against the front of his desk and crossed his arms over his chest. She chose to sit on one of the low-backed, forest green chairs across from the desk.

Frowning, he asked, "Have you ever taken a tour of a factory?"

"No. Have you ever taken a tour of a kitchen?"

"Not yet, but I'm counting on it." He stood and held out his hand. "Let me show you around."

She placed her hand in his and stood. "I'd like that." They were close together—so close she felt his warm breath on her hair. His eyes dropped to her mouth. Heat rose to her cheeks and her pulse beat heavy and thick. Breath was hard to find....

"Virginia..." His voice trailed off.

She parted her lips, then wet them with her tongue.

He groaned, pulling her into his arms and holding her tightly, cradling her head against his shoulder. Every inch of his body was pressed against her, molded against her soft curves.

Her muscles turned liquid, her body forming to his intimately. His mouth claimed hers in a kiss that was as gentle as warm rain, as soft as down and as stirring as being in the arms of the man she loved.

The feel of him, the touch of him, the scent of him...it was a potent blend and she was dizzy with it. With him.

With a wisdom and knowledge that had been there all along but denied, Virginia realized that she loved Wilder Hunnicut. With everything she had. For all the good it would do....

6

VIRGINIA CLOSED HER EYES and held on to Wilder's broad shoulders, allowing herself to sink into the warm, exciting world of touch. Wilder's touch. Her heart raced, keeping pace with his.

His hands roamed her back, molding her to him, feeling her softness. He held her prisoner, and she never wanted to escape—never wanted to think about leaving his side.

Just like a shining beacon in the dark of night, the one phrase that made all this so simple was the one that made it complicated.

I love you.

The accompanying emotions were the only thing that made sense to her. Everything else was minor. She wanted to say the words out loud. Taste them on her tongue, feel the thrill of acknowledgment. She wanted to yell them to people in the hallways, in cars in the parking lot, to anyone and everyone who would listen. For Virginia, love hadn't come up like a slow-moving tide. Instead, it had washed over her like a tidal wave, flattening everything in its path except love itself.

When Wilder began to pull away, she felt bereft. He let go of her, his chest heaving. Her hands slid sensuously down the soft fabric of his shirt, then dropped to her sides. She was embarrassed to think he could see her love for him written on all over her face. That wouldn't do.

Virginia knew she'd been right to keep her revelation to herself when she saw his expression. It was smug.

"I knew it," he said in a voice that resembled a low growl. "I knew you were warm and—"

"Willing?" she questioned. She raised one brow just as he did when he was being patronizing. "Of course. If I hadn't been, you wouldn't have been able to kiss me at all."

He didn't buy the attitude for a moment. "Don't play hard to get with me. You enjoyed it—you felt the same warm feelings I did. You enjoyed it every bit as much."

"Yes. But that doesn't mean—"

This time it was his turn to interrupt. "That you're loose or always willing? Of course not." He smiled and reached up to stroke her bottom lip with his thumb. His tender touch was as erotic as his kiss had been. "You're a different woman than most, Virginia Gallagher. You fascinate me. For the life of me, I can't figure you out."

Hoping her knees would still support her, she took a step back. "And if you did, Mr. Hunnicut—"

"Wilder," he corrected with a smile, showing his slash-mark dimples.

"Wilder...you wouldn't be fascinated any longer. I'd

be history and you'd be kissing someone else behind a closed office door."

"I don't usually kiss women in my office." There was a gentle teasing note in his voice, but she refused to let him get to her.

"A moot point, and not worth pursuing," she pronounced. "But I'd still like a tour of the place—that is, if you're still game. This may be my only chance for it."

"I know," he said. "You're leaving in three or four months."

She smiled sweetly. "You remembered."

He leaned back on his desk and crossed his arms again. But his handsome face was open, his eyes still teasing, and he was clearly enjoying the byplay. "It's keeping track of details that got me where I am today," he joked. Once more he held out his hand. "Would you accompany me on a guided tour of my computer company, Ms. Gallagher?"

Once more she accepted his hand. "I would love to, Mr. Hunnicut," she stated regally.

"Then let's go," he said, tucking her fingers in the crook of his arm. He escorted her to the door, where they parted physically. Emotionally, though, they were still connected, and each look they shared proved it.

THAT NIGHT Virginia made a salad for herself and Mrs. Hunnicut, and they ate in the kitchen. Virginia tried to give no more than cursory answers to the older woman's questions about her tour of the company. Wilder hadn't come home for dinner, and she wondered if it was because he'd decided they'd been too intimate this afternoon. Maybe it was because he'd seen the love in her eyes and known he had to quell it now—for both their sakes.

All through the tour, she'd pretended it was normal and natural for her to be with him, at his side. And yet she knew she wasn't really meant to look like the female half of a couple. It was just her own little fantasy....

She'd felt so proud of being with him, and at the same time she'd felt like a liar. People walked by and stared at her because she was with Wilder. When she was, everyone looked at her differently, silently questioning her position at his side. But it seemed they accepted her.

Virginia only wished Wilder felt the same way. If he did, he certainly hadn't let her know. With every minute that passed, he'd grown more remote, more distant from her. His greeting to all his staff, from the research-and-development department to the installers on the assembly line, had been warm and friendly. He knew several names and more faces. His employees weren't strangers to him. And because of that, they were open and accepting with her, too.

Directly after the tour, Wilder had been called away by a message from Natalie and had excused himself. On the way home Virginia had experienced the heights of heaven and the depths of hell. She'd been treated like a queen, and yet Wilder had slowly but surely withdrawn emotionally. But she'd put on a smile and told him how wonderful everyone was at the plant.

Now she was saying the same things to his mother. However, Mrs. Hunnicut was aware of all that. She'd been to the site many times and knew a surprising amount about her son's business. What Wilder's mother really wanted to know Virginia didn't want to discuss.

"Was my son more human today, my dear?"

Virginia tried to sidestep the issue with laughter. "What does that mean?"

Mrs. Hunnicut wasn't to be deterred. "Did he smile? Joke? Or did he act like he was taking care of some stuffy board member?"

"He was charming." And so was his kiss.

"Well, that's something."

Virginia stood and took her plate to the sink. She hoped Mrs. Hunnicut didn't notice she hadn't eaten much. Her appetite was gone. "Should I make a salad for him and wrap it for later?"

"No," Mrs. Hunnicut replied wearily. "If he was hungry he'll have eaten. Whether I like it or not, he's bound and determined to lead his own life."

"And did you ever think differently?"

"No. But I did hope he'd give me grandchildren before I died. In fact, I wanted to be around so I could spoil them for a few years." She looked even more forlorn. "If he keeps up the way he's going, I'll never get my wish."

Surprised, Virginia turned. "You *wished* for it and it

hasn't come true?" She hadn't expected Mrs. Hunnicut to admit the lamp might not work.

"No. I didn't think to wish on the lamp for it. I took it for granted that Wilder would have children. I made all my wishes before I realized that my son would be too stubborn to fall in love, marry and give me a grand-child before I'm too old to enjoy it!" She looked sad and so very pitiful, but a sudden merry gleam in her eyes gave her away.

Virginia laughed. "Somehow I don't think it has to do with his being stubborn. I think it has more to do with finding the right woman."

Mrs. Hunnicut didn't seem to buy that piece of wis-dom. "Well, almost every eligible woman in several of the largest cities in America have paraded themselves in front of that boy, waiting for him to notice," she said. "And nothing has come of it. Why, I've tried..." She took a bite of her salad and began to chew, as if she hadn't just left her dinner companion hanging on her last words.

"Tried what?" Virginia finally asked.

"Praying. I've tried praying, my dear," Mrs. Hunni-cut said, reaching for another dollop of salad dressing. "So far I haven't had any luck, but I'm still praying for a change."

Virginia doubted the older woman was telling the truth—she hadn't been talking about praying. Preying, maybe. When she'd first found the wallet, Virginia had had the feeling she was being set up. And again later, when she was given the choice of the lamp or the money. In fact, she'd been suspicious several times, but logic had always taken over. After all, Mrs. Hunnicut had been trying to bring her son to the altar for years, and he hadn't made it there yet. Why would she waste her time on a soon-to-be-chef? Especially one who didn't move in her son's sophisticated circle.

If Virginia had felt low earlier, this last thought brought her even lower. Dinner finished, she cleaned up what little mess there was in the kitchen, said good-night to Mrs. Hunnicut, who was reading in the study, and went directly to her room.

She wasn't really sleepy, but she slipped into a V-neck, satin nightdress that barely covered her thighs. Her baby sister, Elizabeth Jean, had sent it as a combination birthday and Christmas gift last year, explaining that it was about time Virginia wore something other than a T-shirt to bed. It was an ongoing joke in her family that the only way Virginia would ever get a man would be to cook for him until he couldn't move, then talk him to death. She silently agreed.

She wasn't flirty enough, didn't own sexy lingerie and was far too independent in her thinking for most men. That reality hadn't bothered her much—until now.

She slipped through the French doors to the balcony and sat on the deck, her back against the side of the house. She took a deep breath and forced herself to re-lax, focusing on the soothing sound of the creek as it bubbled over its limestone bed.

She stared at the full moon and wished on the stars.

Wished that the man she loved loved her. But he didn't love anyone, and it was her guess that he'd never experienced the emotions she was now going through. How sad for both of them.

"Rapunzel, let down your hair," said a masculine voice just as low and gravelly as the sound of the creek below. Virginia looked over the side of the deck and saw Wilder standing below her on another, lower deck.

"Wrong fairy tale. I'm not captive, and my hair's not long enough." Her voice was just above a whisper, but her smile couldn't be contained. He'd come home. Wherever Wilder had gone this evening and whoever he'd been with, he'd come home.

"All right," he said. He took a sip from a short glass and was silent for a minute. Just as Virginia was about to ask how his evening had gone, he looked back up at her. "Snow White, Snow White, get rid of your dwarfs and let me in."

"You, my prince, already have the key," she answered, more seriously than she'd intended.

"And if I used it?" He stared up at her, as serious as she. "What would happen?"

"We don't know, do we?"

"Oh, Snow White," he sighed, sounding sad. "No words of encouragement? No vows of love undying? No recipes for fulfillment?"

"No crystal ball," she retorted softly. "Just my wits and whatever talent the gods gave me."

He tipped his glass in her direction. "I'll drink to

that. Would you like a glass of wine? It will help you sleep better."

"Why? Do I look like an insomniac?"

"It's late and you're not asleep, although you're dressed for it. That speaks for itself."

What was the use denying it—especially to the object of her sleeplessness? "A glass of red wine sounds nice."

"Be right there," he said, finishing his own drink and stepping back inside the house. He'd been on his patio. He was in his room. The thought of him being so close—of him entering her room, stepping onto her balcony—was delicious. Forbidden. Wicked. Wonderful.

Virginia stood up, wondering what the protocol was in this situation. She probably ought to grab a robe, which was great if she'd owned one. Maybe she should change? Into what—daytime clothing? Besides, what she was wearing covered as much as some of her dresses did. What made it feel wicked was the sliplike satin.

"If it's going to be, let it be," she muttered under her breath, never believing that her fantasies could come true.

Her bedroom door opened and Wilder filled the doorway. Light spilled in from the hallway and spread across her bed. He closed the door with his foot and the stream of light disappeared.

She stood at the portal of the French doors, watching, waiting, every muscle tense with anticipation. He strode across the plush carpet, stopping only inches from her, stealing her space with his potent sexuality. She felt his heated gaze down to the tips of her coral-painted toes.

"Do you have any idea how beautiful you are?" When he spoke, she felt his voice brush across her nerves, sending a shiver down her spine, then back up again.

"I don't have any makeup on," she said, blushing.

"You don't need it."

"My hair's a mess."

He glanced at her tousled head. "Perfect."

"I'm barefoot."

His grin was slow, sensuous. Delicious. "Thank God. You're dressed for loving, not for hiking."

She was tingling inside. Her breath was short, her list of needs so long it would fill reams of paper, and they all centered around him. "Is that my wine?"

Wilder looked down at the wineglasses he held as if he'd never seen them before. He stretched out one hand. "Yes. Drink up."

She smiled, taking the glass. "Do you mind if I sip instead?"

"Take your time. I'll anticipate enjoying your every move." His words were loaded with tension, the same tension that was in her. "I was called to a meeting," he continued, "or I would have been here earlier, spending one long, wonderful evening with you and tasting more of those kisses you tempt the gods with."

"My goodness. You are poetic." She couldn't keep the nervousness from her voice.

"We're wasting time," he pronounced. "I want you in my arms as soon as possible."

The wine caught in her throat. "What?" she choked.

His dimples appeared. "Don't pretend you didn't hear or understand me, Virginia. I'm going to hold you, kiss you. Make love to you."

Heat suffused her body, and she dropped her gaze to his hands, then looked back up again, facing him squarely. They were only inches apart, but the threshold of the French doors separated them. That, and several thousand thoughts.

"Is that why you brought me here to work? To make it easier to take me to bed?"

"Not at all. I hired you because I thought you could do the job well and because my mother likes you. It solved both our problems. I want to take you to bed and make love to you because I kissed you and haven't been able to think of a damn thing since then. And I thought you felt the same way."

Such a simple explanation. Direct and to the point. This was the time to say yes or no.

"I do," she replied.

His gaze was hard as stone, only now she knew the harshness for what it was—a defense. He was waiting for answers, and this was his way of protecting himself in case it wasn't the response he wanted. "You do what?" he demanded.

"I do want to make love with you."

The tension eased a little. "That wasn't the question," he said. "I'd already figured that part out. What I want to know *now* is if you will. Tonight."

"Yes. Yes. Yes."

Wilder took the glass from her hand and sat it on the dresser beside his own. Then he looked back to where she stood in the light of the full moon.

He held out his arms. "Come here."

She raised both brows, pretending she was in control when she couldn't even find her breath. "Do you often order women around?"

"All the time. But not usually in these circumstances." She knew his patience was over. He wasn't willing to play games.

His hand snaked out and clasped her wrist, gently but firmly pulling her into his arms. He stopped drawing her close when her soft breasts met the hardness of his chest. With satisfaction lacing his mouth, he placed one of her hands on his shoulder. "Touch me," he said. "Don't be afraid."

Circling his arms around her waist, he placed his hands possessively on her hips, holding her tightly. Her hand was clenched in a fist of denial on his shoulder, but her grip loosened into submissiveness and she began to stroke and soothe the muscles in his neck.

When his mouth covered hers she felt as if he was in possession of all of her. His tongue danced erotically inside her mouth; his lips were soft, firm, full. He confirmed what she'd known all along—that he was the best kisser she'd ever known. He deserved an award, a medal, and a wonderful night of love in appreciation.

He could have been with anyone at all, but he'd come home, instead. He'd chosen her.

Virginia's heart overflowed. She held his head in her hands and tried to show him how she felt by kissing him back with all the love in her.

He moaned again, his blood pulsing through his veins so strongly she could feel it under her palms. She was causing this reaction in him. Only her and no one else. She felt heady with sensuality. Wilder made her feel as if she were the most feminine of women, as if any movement she made would be sexy, flowing. So very right. It made her feel very brave.

Eyes wide in the moonlight, she stared up at him as he pulled away. "What do you do when women give *you* orders?" she asked, her voice a hoarse whisper. "Or is this a one-way street?"

His gaze narrowed on her. "What did you have in mind?"

She glanced at him through her lashes, then back to his chest. "Take off your shirt."

His nostrils flared. "Now?"

"Is there a better time?" she asked provocatively, pulling on his already loosened tie and dropping it to the floor.

He let go of her and she swayed a little without his hands holding her. Her lids dropped as she watched his movements, which were quick, sure and impatient.

Once Wilder's shirt was completely unbuttoned, he

pulled it from his pants and let it hang open. Then he undid his black, lizard-skin belt, unhooked and unzipped his suit pants. Wilder placed his hands on his hips and stared down at her, his hunger apparent. There was a daring look in his eyes.

"Enough?"

"Not enough," she said slowly. "More."

"Not until you take off that satin thing so I can see the real you." His voice was harsh; his gaze seared her with a heat so strong she could barely continue to stand in front of him and feel the full blast. "Either you take it off or I will."

"Why take it off at all?" She was flirting with danger, and she loved it. She loved the man, why not love the dangerous mood he was in?

"Virginia..." he growled.

Still she goaded him. "Take it off, Wilder. You first."

He shoved down his slacks and shorts until they dropped to the floor.

The little gasp that passed her lips caused the tension to ease from his face. She stared, unable to stop herself.

"I think you've made your intention clear," she finally managed to say in a hoarse whisper.

"Now you do the same," he said. "Slowly."

"I'm not a show stopper," she demurred.

"In whose eyes?" His gaze never wavered. He didn't expect an answer, she didn't give one. His next word was a command. "*Now.*"

As if her will belonged to someone else, she obeyed. She'd always been tall and slim, but right now she felt as if her body was willowy and supple—beautiful and wanting to be loved.

It wasn't until she found the nerve to look up that she realized her opinion about her body wasn't the one that counted here. He was staring down at her, his eyes sexy and deep. She held her breath as she waited for him to say something, anything.

"My God," Wilder finally murmured, reaching out. That said it all for Virginia. She no longer felt shy or uncertain. His next words confirmed her emotions. "You're so beautiful."

He pulled her back into his arms. Flesh met flesh; hair-roughened chest rubbed against the softness of pouting nipples, sending electric shocks through the rest of her body. She swayed in his arms, aware of some intimate music that seemed to sing through her veins.

Once more he kissed her and once more she succumbed, releasing inhibitions to the wind—releasing herself to Wilder.

As he pulled away to gaze upon her once more, she took his hand and led him to the bed. "Don't you think it's about time we made use of this thing?"

"Past time," he said, shedding the rest of his clothing as she lay down. Within a second he was at her side, holding, kissing her breasts with his moist, hot mouth and making her squirm in delight.

"Touch me," he whispered. "I need you to hold and touch me, too."

And she did, tentatively at first, then with more bravado. She loved the feel of him—all of him. He was strong and masculine and very, very, hard.

When he covered her with his body, she was ready. He entered and filled her up. At the moment, there was no one—nothing—as important. Her body couldn't hold her ecstasy for another moment.

With a sweet cry that came from somewhere deep inside, she exploded with overwhelming emotions. Rainbow sensations followed one after another, transporting her to a place she'd never been before. Afraid she was falling off the edge of the earth, she managed to cling to Wilder's broad back, using him as an anchor.

From far away, she heard his satisfied laugh. Then, with a thrust, he stiffened, groaned and buried his head in the curve of her neck. His warm breath fanned against her throat and shoulder. Virginia held on to him, immersed in her own feelings still but unwilling to let go of the man she had just loved.

Their breath raced in unison, heartbeat fluttering against heartbeat. She felt him kiss her shoulder and gave a happy sigh.

He pulled back. "You were terrific. You know that?"

She smiled, her eyes still closed and her body still floating on a soft cloud. "Mmm. Thank you, boss."

Then he pulled away, leaving her breasts and belly chilled. "No, darlin'. Thank *you*."

She propped herself up by her elbows and ran her fingers through her tousled hair. She didn't want to think what she was thinking. She didn't want to feel the abandonment she was feeling. This wasn't how it was supposed to be after making beautiful love with the one you adore. "Where are you going?"

"I've got some paperwork to finish," he muttered, slipping into his pants, then throwing on his shirt in the dark. He leaned over and gave her a chaste kiss on her slightly parted mouth. "But I thank you for such a...wonderful diversion."

Virginia felt chilled to the bone. "I see."

Wilder picked up his shoes and socks and walked to the door. "I knew you'd understand. Good night, Virginia."

Knowing the hall light was shining on her face, she hid her cold thoughts with a warm smile. He would not find out how much this hurt. She blinked quickly. He would never know. "Good night, Wilder. Pleasant dreams."

7

VIRGINIA HELD HIS PILLOW against her stomach and curled into a ball, silently crying herself into numbness. Her heart ached with a hurt so heavy she could hardly bear the weight of it. Wilder had used her, then left as if she were no more than a receptacle. Another sob choked her.

Although losses could last forever, tears couldn't. Neither could feeling sorry for herself.

As used as she felt, she knew better. Wilder hadn't committed a crime. He'd only taken what had been generously, openly offered. No, he hadn't committed a crime.

It had been her fantasy, not his, that had been fulfilled—almost. Just because she loved him and wanted to make love with him didn't necessarily mean he felt the same way. Obviously he didn't love her in return, or after lovemaking he would have held her close, stroked her, whispered in her ear all those wonderful, delicious things she craved to hear.

But he had done none of that. Instead, he'd left her side immediately, fleeing from her on rapid wings.

Her heart was broken and her ego crushed.

All night long Virginia tossed and turned, reliving

the last minutes of their time together. Was there anything she could have done differently that would have
changed the outcome? Would she ever be able to face
him again or should she run away now? If she ran
away, what would she do? Find another job? Go back
to the diner? Get an apartment?

Somewhere around early morning, she knew what
she had to do if she was going to live through the next
three-and-a-half months. Just because last night had
gone wrong didn't mean everything was wrong. She
boiled it down to a few points: she loved Wilder; he
didn't love her. She'd made love to him and he'd made
love to her. She was no worse off now than *before* she'd
made love to him. She had expected him to have some
sort of cosmic realization of his deep and abiding feelings for her. She had fantasized that everything would
change when he held her in his arms. Apparently, that
only happened in love stories and songs. This was reality.

Nothing had changed. She realized now that he
didn't have a clue about her feelings. He'd been too
wrapped up in himself to see her. Relief flooded her
heated body. Nothing had changed.

She could walk into breakfast in the morning and
smile, and aside from feeling embarrassed about their
intimacy and his fleeing her bedroom as if he was being chased, she could pretend it had never happened.
No one would be the wiser. No one would know just
what a fool she'd been!

Tears for the loss of her love continued to roll down

her cheeks, but her pride, although battered and bruised, felt somewhat better.

Her acting skills were going to be tested beyond belief....

WILDER STOOD IN FRONT OF his mirror and attempted for the third time to put a double Windsor knot in his tie. He didn't look himself in the eye. He couldn't.

He'd spent half the night kicking and cursing himself for what he'd done with Virginia. Logic and a deep sense of guilt told him he never should have taken her to bed. He felt worse than he'd ever felt in his life.

Finally, he stared at his reflection and tried to lie. Temporary insanity—that's what it had been. Pure lust and temporary insanity...

But for all of one minute after making love to her he'd felt so good, so happy, so contented....

Then he'd run like the guilty coward he was. He'd faced Congress, international competitors, his board of directors. He'd faced and fought them until he'd won. Those, however, were visible foes; there was something tangible to conquer.

He was way out of his element when it came to sweet, sexy, delectable Virginia.

Wilder mumbled an expletive under his breath and pulled at the misshapen knot. He began to redo his tie for the fourth time.

If there had been any way to erase what had happened last night, he would have done it. As it was, though, it was too late. Now his only recourse was to act like an adult and own up to one hell of a huge mistake.

His conscience mocked him. He'd *really* blown it. When he should have been feeling ashamed of himself for taking advantage of Virginia, he didn't want to pretend it never happened. He wanted to remember it, savor it, wallow in the wonderful feelings of release and peace, which was the main reason he felt guilty....

Good knot or not, it was time to halt the stall tactics. By sheer determination, Wilder walked out of his bedroom and down the hall to the dining room. Morning sunshine poured across the table, reflecting off the white walls of the room and making it feel as sunny as orange juice. He stepped in, his heart sinking as he realized both Virginia and his mother were already up, dressed and in the middle of breakfast. For the first time in a long time, he wished his mother was well enough to move back to her own home.

She looked up, smiling. Slowly, her smile turned to an expression of parental concern. "My goodness, Wilder. You look as if you haven't slept a wink! Are you feeling all right?"

He felt Virginia's gaze on him, but he couldn't look at her yet. One problem at a time. "I'm fine." His tone was curt, but he softened it with a smile. "I have a headache."

"Isn't that supposed to be a woman's malady?" Virginia's soft voice interposed.

Was that laughter in her voice? His eyes were drawn in her direction. She stood by his mother's side, the calendar notebook she used for appointments in her hands. Yes, there was a definite smile on her lips, and that easy, bright smile was directed at him. His tension began to ease a little.

"Women don't have an exclusive on headaches," he said tersely, and realized he still needed to ease up. "Just the right to talk about it."

"So sorry you're feeling badly," Virginia said, and this time there was no mistaking the laugher lurking in her tone. He hated that smugness. It was the kind that said, *You poor stupid male. It's a shame you're not as intelligent, witty, sharp as I am. I am female.*

Here he'd been worried all night about taking advantage of poor, sweet, innocent Virginia, when that sweet innocence must be only skin-deep. There was no other way to explain how, in two short minutes of conversation, she'd gotten the upper hand in their relationship—such as it was.

He walked over to the sidebar and poured himself a cup of coffee, doctoring it with cream and sugar. He normally took it black, but this wasn't a normal morning. "You certainly seem chipper today. Feeling fine, are you?"

"Wonderful," she said brightly. "Ready to conquer the day and the kitchen. And you? Did you have a good night's sleep?" She slid gracefully into her usual seat beside his mother and looked up at him inquiringly, as if she didn't have a care in the world.

"No." It was all he intended to say on the subject. She could gloat some other time. He reached for a bagel and lavishly spread cream cheese and orange marmalade over it, then bit into it as if he held manna from heaven.

"How was your meeting last night?" his mother asked.

"Meeting?" An image of Virginia's soft, sweet flesh popped into his head—her beautiful breasts and pouting nipples, her skin as creamy as morning milk. Her sexy little sounds echoed in his ear once more.

"Yes. That *was* why you weren't here for dinner after saying you would be?" his mother persisted.

"Yes. Sorry." Wilder gulped down his coffee and put the cup on the table. "I'm late for work." He stood and turned to go. "See you all later." Except for the first bite, his bagel remained untouched. He wasn't hungry anymore.

"Oh, Wilder?" Virginia said, and her voice stopped him in his tracks. "Have a wonderful day."

He stole a look at her and saw nothing but genuine caring. No intimacy. No hint at tears and recriminations. Nothing. "Thanks," he mumbled, and strode out of the room. He picked up his briefcase and walked out the door, then waited impatiently for Sammy to get the van.

But all the while, there was a sense of relief Wilder hadn't expected. Virginia wasn't making a scene. Apparently, she wasn't anxious to draw and quarter him; she wasn't even slightly angered by his behavior last night. And she certainly hadn't acted possessive or clinging. In fact, if he didn't know better, he'd say she didn't care.

Another thought came to mind. Maybe she wasn't interested in him at all. Maybe he was such a bad lover she didn't care whether or not she ever saw him again. Maybe last night didn't mean anything to her.

That final thought unsettled him more than any other.

VIRGINIA WORKED HARD in cooking school, centering all her concentration on a new recipe featuring pear cactus. Her head instructor, Charlie Feather, one of the finest Southwest chefs in the country, came up behind her.

"Great presentation. How's it going?"

"Fine," she said. "Wish I could do this for a living."

He laughed, his lined face birthing more wrinkles. "And you will as soon as you're out of here." He rested his hand on her shoulder. "You're my star Virginia. I have great dreams for you. Just hang in there and good things will come to pass. Eventually."

His praise didn't come often, but it was always sincere. She flashed him a smile. "Thanks. Now, if I can just live up to your expectations..."

He gave her shoulder a squeeze. "Ease up on yourself. You already have."

He moved on and Virginia went back to her work, making minor adjustments to the strips of cactus before adding the light green avocado sauce. But her concentration was broken because with every second thought, she remembered Wilder.

She placed another strip of cactus on the plate, adding to the starburst design. She recalled how Wilder's hands had memorized her body's curves....

Virginia shook those thoughts off and stirred the sauce. As she did she felt the weight of his lean, supple body against hers....

She placed a grilled chicken breast on the side of the plate next to the cactus and remembered him leaving so quickly after they'd made love. She'd felt so sad at first, not understanding how insecure he was, making love with a woman with whom he also had a business relationship. It had been a spur-of-the-moment thing for him, and Virginia had a feeling that Wilder hadn't done too many things for fun or pleasure on the spur of the moment.

That thought brought a smile to her face.

Since that unforgettable morning two weeks ago she'd played it so easy. They'd gone back to being friends and employer/employee and that was fine. The sexual tension between them was still like an invisible wall, but neither acknowledged it or bridged it or fed it.

At least he'd relaxed a little since that episode, which was something. Occasionally they even enjoyed their old relationship of bantering and baiting....

She was satisfied with that. Virginia took her plate and joined the others at the bar, waiting for judging to begin. She tried to concentrate on the goings-on, but her mind was still working on two levels. She needed to pay attention to what was happening. The competition was stiff, and this was her profession, after all.

Finally, when it was over, her mentor and teacher came to her. "Congratulations," he said, "you've done it again. A superb effort and equal to anything I could do."

She smiled. "Really?"

"Really. You have surpassed yourself, my Irish rose. Congratulations again."

It finally dawned on her that Charlie Feather was telling more than he was saying. She narrowed her eyes, searching his lined face. "Okay, Charles, what exactly are you telling me?"

"That two of our esteemed guest judges today own restaurants in Dallas. They both expressed interest in you."

"Oh, my," she whispered. "Which restaurants?"

"I cannot say until they make their move, Irish. Then I'll get you together." He smiled. "But don't worry, you are wonderful. Just keep paying attention to your esteemed teacher's advice."

Excitement bubbled up inside her as she realized he was talking about opportunities with some of the best restaurants in Texas. If they weren't the best, Charles Feather wouldn't be so satisfied with himself and her. She was on her way to being the success she'd wished to be. She knew it!

The memory of the night when she'd made her first wish on the magic lamp came back in detail. She'd asked for money and career. And it looked as if she'd gotten both.

All the way home, she was making a mental list of the things she would do with her first paycheck.

She would find a different car. One that didn't need a constant supply of bailing wire and bubble gum to keep it running. Yes, that was a number-one priority.

She'd get a haircut. What a treat to have a *style* she hadn't given herself! Something that flattered her instead of just ensuring that her hair didn't hang in her eyes!

And maybe she'd buy a few pieces of brand-new clothing. She didn't mind looking like a secondhand rose some of the time. In fact, sometimes she liked to look retro-sixties, but not all the time. There were special occasions when she wanted to be sophisticated and *pretty*.

By the time Virginia parked her ancient jalopy outside the garage, she was so excited she practically bounced out of the car.

Standing next to the garage doors, Sammy grinned. "Looks like you had one heck of a day."

"I did. My teacher just told me I'm being scouted by two—count 'em, two—" she held up two fingers for emphasis, "—restaurants in Dallas!" She did a quick dance, waltzing with a ghostly partner. "It's the best news I've had since I went back to school."

Sammy laughed. Taking her hands, he placed them on his shoulders and danced with her. "Just watching you makes me feel happy," he said. "We'll do this again when *my* grades come in."

"You're doing well?"

"No, but I won't fail. That's something to dance about, don't you think?"

She laughed again. "Of course it is! Anything good is worth dancing about!"

Sammy joined in the laughter, then gave her a giant hug. "Congratulations."

"Is this a private dance or can anyone join in?"

Wilder stood at the side of the driveway, hands in the pockets of his tuxedo pants. Virginia and Sammy stopped in their tracks and stared at him—their employer. He was obviously on his way to some exclusive engagement with—some exclusive female. Virginia felt her cheeks flush, but she refused to pull away from Sammy. It was Sammy who retreated, dropping his arms and taking several steps back.

Virginia gave a mock curtsy. "It's a private party, but you're certainly welcome to join. Who knows, you might give this joint a little class." She looked around the open area of the driveway, then purposely hesitated, raised one brow and added, "Sir." She wanted to remind him that she and Sammy were employees; he was the boss. She also hoped it made Wilder realize that he had not been intimate with her for a long time. Two whole weeks.

Sammy moved toward the garage door, opened it by punching in the code on a keypad. The door lifted and Sammy was gone in seconds.

Wilder ignored him. "What's the occasion?"

Even though Virginia was thrown off guard by his appearance, she couldn't keep her enthusiasm from showing. Perhaps he'd forgotten that night two weeks ago, and perhaps she should, too. "I was told that two different restaurants are vying for an interview."

"With you?"

"Of *course* with me!" She laughed. "I wouldn't be half this excited if it was with one of my fellow chefs."

Wilder didn't even crack a smile. "When?"

Virginia shrugged. "I don't know. Probably within a week of graduating." She tilted her head and stared up at him. "You could be a little happier for me, you know," she said softly.

His harsh expression eased somewhat as he gave a small smile. "I'm happy for you. I just didn't expect those damn scouts to be looking so soon."

"Luckily, those 'damn scouts' are always looking." Her buoyant mood was returning. Even Wilder couldn't change that. "If they weren't they might pass up wonderful finds—like me!"

Wilder finally managed to say the words she wanted to hear, even if they were stated grudgingly. "Congratulations on your success. You deserve it."

"Thank you. But I haven't had an interview yet."

"I'm sure you will. You're too determined to succeed not to be chosen."

Virginia chuckled. "You don't have to make it sound like it's a *bad* thing."

"Sorry." He headed toward the garage again. "Good

luck." Just as he reached the sedan, he turned and looked at her, staring back at him. "If you're up later, I'd like to help you celebrate with a glass of wine and a few good toasts."

She smiled slowly. "I'd like that."

Wilder finally lightened up. "Good. I'll see you around ten tonight," he said with some enthusiasm.

Virginia watched him drive away. It wasn't until the sound of his engine was only a distant murmur that she let loose with a cheer.

What a wonderful day!

WILDER'S FINGERS WERE white from clutching the wheel so tightly. He took another deep breath and eased his foot off the accelerator, bringing the speedometer down to a reasonable seventy.

Purposely, he eased the tension between his shoulders, telling himself that it was only the end of a very long and difficult day that had brought on this feeling of extreme jealousy.

When he'd discovered Virginia in Sammy's arms, an animal urge so strong came over him that for a moment he couldn't see or hear. He'd had to take several deep breaths and tell himself to calm down before the muscles in his throat unlocked and allowed him to speak. Meanwhile, he'd stood silently, helplessly, watching another man circle the driveway with the woman he... He what? Lusted after? Craved until it ate at him like a searing pain in his gut? Wanted in his bed in spite of knowing it wasn't right?

His fist hit the steering wheel. "What, damn it! What is she?"

Just another woman, he told himself, but he knew better. If she was just another woman, he'd be able to wave goodbye to her just as easily as he had all the rest.

So what the hell was she? He'd asked himself that very question for almost two weeks and he wasn't any closer to an answer now that he'd ever been.

He wanted to possess her. He wanted to say she belonged to him. He wanted her enthusiasm and her laughter. His thirst for her was overwhelming. He craved her.

It wasn't love, he reassured himself. He'd had experience with that emotion and it was different: love was cloying and demanding. Love was a woman wanting him to pay constant attention to her wants and needs— he'd run into a few women who thought they loved him, and that's how it always went.

Okay, so that left the animal urge to procreate.

No, that wasn't right. No matter how hard he tried to believe it, Virginia wasn't just a biological urge. She was sweet and smart and had a smile that hit his heart like a hammer. He'd known he wanted her the moment he'd seen that smile. He'd pretended otherwise, but that was the truth.

And he didn't want his chauffeur anywhere near her. He didn't want *any* man near her.

Didn't she understand they had something special in bed that didn't come around too often in life? Damn it! Did he have to explain it to her?

The answer was yes. She simply needed to know his ground rules for their affair. And then he could have her.

"I HAVE A BOTTLE of champagne if you want to celebrate." Wilder spoke softly into the warm night, but Virginia heard every sound, every nuance, from his balcony to hers. She looked down to see him standing there in the moon-light. He was wearing a tuxedo, his bow tie undone, and he held a bottle in one hand, two glasses in the other.

"Bring it up," Virginia whispered. "Although I would have settled for beer."

"Forget it." He grinned. "It's first class or no class at all."

"Bring it up, then," she whispered again. Knowing he was home and hadn't forgotten his earlier promise made her feel as if fine wine already flowed through her veins.

Moments later, he stepped out to her balcony and placed the glasses on the railing.

"Good evening, Ms. Chef. What else have you done to celebrate tonight?" he asked. His gaze was piercing and she could see moonbeams reflected in his eyes.

"Your mother and I had an extra glass of wine after dinner."

"And Sammy?"

Warning bells went off in her head. "What about Sammy?"

"Did you celebrate with him?"

"Is that any of your business?" she asked softly.

"Yes."

She wasn't going to give in gracefully. These questions were coming from a man who never explained his own whereabouts, yet he wanted to account for hers?

Her back stiffened. Once upon a time, she would have answered without a thought. But not anymore. He'd left her bed and hadn't returned. He no longer had any rights to her private life. "How did you become involved with my celebration?"

"Because we've slept together. Because I need to make a few things clear if we're to continue."

He had the grace to fiddle with the cork, his attention and gaze elsewhere.

"Continue? Continue what?"

The cork gave a satisfying pop.

"Don't play coy, Virginia." He poured the champagne, his gaze locked on the glasses. "I'm just trying to ensure that we're safe, as well as intimate."

"That's funny, coming from someone who makes love, runs out and isn't seen for the next two weeks."

He handed her a bubbling glass, then picked up his own. His attitude and voice were casual, easy. But she saw a thread of wariness in his gaze. "You thought it was a one-night stand."

"My first clue was when you never returned. My second clue was when you acted as if you didn't know or care about me any more than you do..." she searched for a word, then decided on a person "...Sammy."

Wilder stiffened at the name. "Which brings me to my original question. What about Sammy?"

Her chin came up and she stared Wilder straight in the eye. "My relationship with Sammy is none of your business. You haven't earned the right to question me on my personal life any more than I have to question yours."

Wilder winced at the truth of her words. "Ouch." He leaned against the rail. "You really know how to hurt a man."

She sipped her drink, wishing she hadn't pressed for this discussion. She had another wish, too. She wished she had the nerve to state what she really wanted to know, which was where he had been tonight and all the other nights they hadn't been together, and with whom. "Truth does that, doesn't it?"

He didn't answer. Crickets chirped, an occasional owl hooted its hunting song and water trickled musically over limestone, making its own music, but between them stretched silence.

At long last Wilder spoke. "I'm a silent partner in a new country club. We had the private gala opening tonight."

She took another sip. Her glass was almost empty. "Sounds nice."

"I went alone."

She looked up at him, her heart suddenly light and airy. "I haven't seen Sammy since you left tonight. In fact, that was the first time I'd seen him in three days, when he last took your mother to the doctor."

His expression eased. "Can we start again?"

Relief flooded her body, all the way down to her curled toes. "I'd love to."

He sighed, then stared at her, his gaze open and honest. "Virginia, I want your arms around me. I need to hold you and forget the outside world for a little while."

She balanced her glass carefully on the railing, then turned to stand just inches from him. She looked into his eyes, took a shaky deep breath and got the question out. "Are you two-timing me, Wilder? Is there someone else in the picture?"

"No. Since you've come into my life there hasn't been anyone else." He touched her cheek, then followed the line of her jaw down to her throat; he put his finger on the pulse that beat erratically in the hollow. "And you?"

"There hasn't been anyone for a very long time. Since way before I moved to Austin," she said softly. Her arms lightly circled his waist. "And then you came along."

"And now?"

She knew what Wilder was asking. He was seeking confirmation that Sammy and she hadn't been together. It showed that he cared more than he was saying, and that gave her an exciting, warm feeling. "There's still no one but you."

He placed his own glass next to hers and slipped his

arms around her hips, tugging her closer to fit her curves to his hardness. "Now that we've gotten the trivia out of the way," he said, suddenly light and teasing, "can I interest you in a night of carnal desire?"

"I'm not sure." She tilted her head inquisitively. "My boss needs me early tomorrow. Do you think we could call it quits at half a night of carnal desire?"

"Tell your boss to take his job and shove it. You have to have a personal life."

She smiled up at him. "I'll do that. But if he fires me, you're in trouble."

"I'll take that chance," Wilder stated before claiming her mouth with his own.

Virginia was back where she wanted to be, in Wilder's arms. She only wished he loved her as much as she loved him.

Maybe in time...

A small sadness crept into her heart. She knew delusions weren't good for the soul. And if Wilder loved her, she would know it.

He *wanted* her, but there was a vast difference wanting and loving. But at least he was on the right track, and maybe in time...

8

THIS TIME after making passionate love to Virginia, Wilder did not leave her. This time he held her close far into the night. This time he whispered how much he loved to make love to her. It wasn't the same as saying he loved her, but it was a start.

Virginia sighed, stroking his side as she burrowed her face into his lightly furred chest. His low purr told her he enjoyed the feeling as much as she did.

"You're very special," he rumbled.

"Thank you," she said softly, wishing she could say the words that sat on the tip of her tongue and itched to be spoken aloud. "You're special, too."

"Really? How?"

She kissed the tip of his chin. "How many men do you know who have started a company from scratch and done so well so quickly?" she asked.

"Hundreds."

"See what I mean?" She burrowed back against his chest and dropped a light kiss there, too. "There are millions of people in the United States alone and there are thousands of businesses started every year. Only hundreds succeed for a year, less than that number for longer. Your business succeeded. I rest my case."

His laughter was like thunder in his chest and vibrated against her mouth. "You're wonderful," he said. "Remind me to talk to you before a board meeting."

"Will do," she said, unwilling to yawn, but unable to stop herself.

He kissed her temple lightly. "Poor, sweet baby. I've worn you out." His arms tightened around her. "Sleep. We'll talk tomorrow."

"When will I see you again?"

"Tomorrow night." He kissed the top of her head. "You didn't *really* think I'd let you go that easily, did you?"

"I was hoping not," Virginia admitted with a heartfelt sigh against his warm chest. She took a deep breath and inhaled the scent of him, filling herself with it. It felt so right to be in his arms—as if she'd waited all her life for this moment. She prayed he felt the same way.

This was heaven. Right here in his arms. "I'll see you at breakfast," he said, withdrawing his arms and leaving her, once again, bereft. He pulled away completely, but Virginia felt his reluctance and wondered why he was leaving if he didn't want to go. She didn't have enough nerve to ask.

Wilder leaned over and kissed her parted lips. "I'll see you tomorrow," he promised. "Sleep well."

Virginia finally found her nerve. "Why are you leaving?"

"Because I still have some paperwork to do. I have a

board meeting tomorrow morning and it's important enough to warrant homework."

Virginia felt better knowing he wasn't running just to run, but she still wanted to be with him. "Can I help?"

He flashed a smile. "Not now. Maybe next time."

So there would be another time. She smiled back. "I'll be here if you change your mind," she said in a husky voice.

His laughter was low and sexy, and echoed through her body. "I'll remember," he promised.

Then he was gone.

Virginia lay in bed staring at the ceiling for a long time. She loved him. She knew it. But she needed to know he loved her, too.

With a quick, fluid movement, she bounded from the bed and opened her closet. By the light of the moon and stars, she carefully took the ancient lamp from its box. Then, with hands that shook with excitement, she lit the wick and made her second wish.

"Please let the man who loves me most enter my life so I can love him back easily and freely," she whispered. "I guess what I'm asking for is to live happily ever after with the man who loves me and wants to be with me forever."

With a light heart, she blew out the lamp, then carefully replaced it in its small box and put it away. She went to bed and slept, knowing the spirits-that-be would take care of her wish for Wilder to love her.

It wasn't until she awoke the next morning that she

realized she had goofed big-time. She hadn't mentioned Wilder's name. In a way, she'd done it on purpose, hoping not to jinx the wish process with particulars. But now she knew she'd been wrong. She should have asked for Wilder to love her as she loved him. Mrs. Hunnicut had told her to be sure of what she asked for and to pay close attention to her wording. Instead, she'd rushed ahead without forethought and asked for the wrong thing, putting her wish into words that would have no meaning to anyone but herself.

Did this mean she should make her last wish, and do it right this time?

A feeling from deep inside told her no. She had to trust. She had to trust.

Of course, all this was speculation, Virginia sternly reminded herself. It all depended upon whether or not she truly believed in the power of the lamp to grant wishes. *Wilder* didn't, but his mother believed right down to her bones that the lamp was magical.

Despite her panic, Virginia would wait and see. Her first wish had already come true, so she had reason to lean toward believing....

WILDER WALKED OUT OF the office with a lightness in his step he hadn't experienced in years; he was looking forward to going home. It had been a month since he'd come to an agreement with Virginia. And now she was so much a part of his home life he couldn't imagine her not being there.

Of course, he told himself, he wasn't any more at-

tached to Virginia than to any other good friend and
lover. And they *were* good friends. Holding her in his
arms in the dark of night, he talked to her about everything that was going on in his life—problems that
hounded him or funny incidents. She listened and
laughed, and occasionally made a suggestion—a *good*
suggestion.

In turn, she shared a little of her life in cooking
school. She told him humorous stories and gave in-
sights into people he didn't know but, thanks to her de-
scriptions, became well-rounded characters who engaged his interest.

Yes, he was content with his life and Virginia's role
in it. He also appreciated her hard work in keeping his
personal affairs and his mother's in order and separate
from his business. His mother was happy to have
someone else dealing with her appointments and problems. Sammy was happy because he knew in advance
what his schedules were. And Wilder was happy because Virginia worked so well with Natalie that it
made his life easier.

He waved at the receptionist on his way out and
sauntered to his car. He'd driven himself today, so that
he could stop off at the country club for a drink with a
senator from Dallas. After that, he'd be on his way
home. At the thought of Virginia waiting for him his
foot pressed a little heavier on the gas.

"WHERE IS SHE?" he asked, trying not to sound as if he
was demanding an answer, when in fact he was.

Mrs. Hunnicut looked surprised at the question. "Why, I don't know, dear. Virginia doesn't explain what she does on her free time. And I don't ask." She looked up at her son's stormy face. "And why would *you?*"

"We were going to discuss a few appointments I'd set up for the week," Wilder managed to reply. He was unwilling to admit, even to himself, just how disappointed he was. He wanted to see her. Now. He'd waited all day to bask in her smile and warm laughter. He'd come home early. Damn it, she should be here. Or she should have said something to someone. Damn it! She should have said something to him!

"If you leave them with me, I'll make sure she adds them to her event calendar."

"That's all right, Mom. I'll wait." He poured two glasses of wine and silently offered his mother one. She accepted.

"You're not getting...involved with Virginia, are you, dear? You know she's not like the other women you date." His mother gazed up at him, wide-eyed. She'd been reading when he came in, and the book lay in her lap, cover side up. It was a romance, he could tell.

"Involved what way?" he countered.

His mother ignored his question. "She's got spunk and spirit," she said, "and intelligence and ambition— and that ambition isn't aimed at hooking you as a husband so she can get a free ride through life as a social-ite."

Wilder nodded toward the book that rested on her lap. "You've been reading too many of those stories, Mom. I think your imagination is taking flight."

"Be thankful I don't read mysteries, Wilder," she retorted dryly. "Or the written word might tempt me to murder you in frustration."

"I know your technique, Mom. You throw a pretty girl in my way and hope I'll rise to the bait."

"You know, Wilder, I don't need to read. All I have to do is listen to your fairy tales. You have imagination enough for both of us."

He ignored her comment. "You don't want me to find the woman of my choice, you want to pick the woman of *your* choice. You must have something against me."

"At least I'd *pick* one. I wouldn't walk around alone in an ivory tower and wonder why I'm not married and giving my dear mother grandchildren to bounce on her knee."

"What would you have me do?"

"I'd have you find someone to care for who cares for you. Personally," she added emphatically. "Your problem is that you think the right woman is going to drop from the sky and mold herself to your life-style so you can go about your business and be with her when you feel like it, ignore her when you don't."

"The perfect wife," he answered, knowing that reply would set his mother's teeth on edge.

"Tell me the truth, Wilder," she said placidly,

thoughtfully, surprising him. "Just what do you think of our Virginia?"

He stared down at his mother. Her face was shining with inquisitiveness, but he didn't see any diabolical scheming or manipulating, through he knew it was there.

"I agree with you, Mother. I think 'our Virginia' is a very nice, very competent, very intelligent and very ambitious young woman. I'm glad we hired her and I'm glad she's here for the next month or so. Does that answer your question?"

"Not well enough," she muttered in disgust. "Have a nice evening, son. You're too dull for me. I'm going back to my reading." She looked up hopefully. "Unless you'd like to play a few games of gin? Penny a point?"

"Not tonight, Mom." He smiled absently. "Maybe another time."

He left his glass of wine untouched and went to his room, feeling restless and on edge. Stripping out of his suit, Wilder slipped on a pair of worn shorts and sandals and headed out the patio door, taking the stairs two at a time to the bottom. He needed to get out and stretch his legs, look at something besides four walls and a mother who nagged—even if he did agree with her.

Moments later, he was walking in the creek, feeling the icy spring water sloshing against his ankles. He used to come this way a lot when he'd first moved here, enjoying the serenity of nature, allowing the scenery to soothe his spirits.

As always, it worked, soothing all his thoughts except one: where in the everlasting hell was Virginia Gallagher?

He seemed to gravitate toward the old cave his mother and father had visited on so many occasions. His father had used it as a background to the story of the small clay lamp he'd held so dear. While Wilder was in college he'd seen a similar lamp in a Greek exposition. When he'd mentioned it to his father, the older man had winked and said he'd heard there were others wandering around, and wasn't it wonderful that the Greeks had visited our shores and taught the North Americans a thing or two. From that point on Wilder had taken the magic with a big grain of salt. His father, for whatever reason, might even have planted the lamp in the now-closed cave so he could present it to his bride as a fantasy gift.

Nevertheless, his mother's deep faith in the lamp's power had never wavered. And strange as it seemed even after his heart attack, his father's belief matched his mother's. Could his dad *really* have forgotten that the lamp wasn't real?

On the other hand, maybe his father truly needed to believe in something that seemed so fanciful now.

That thought caught Wilder by surprise. He'd never questioned the meaning behind his father's wink until Virginia stepped into his life. But the more involved he became with her, the more he didn't want her to be hurt by thinking the lamp would do something miraculous for her. He was uncomfortable with the thought of being part of something that would disappoint her.

She was so proud, so independent. He couldn't bring himself to step on those traits. He'd tried to warn her on several occasions, but the dreamer in her was just like the dreamer in his mother. She wanted to believe—and so she did.

He couldn't make her understand without crushing that wonderful, creative spirit she had, her naive innocence....

A beaten and rocky path overrun with short, prickly shrubs wound up the side of the bluff. Wilder stopped, hands on his hips, and stared at the shallow cave above him, the cave where his father had found the magic lamp—if it *was* magic. Wilder hadn't been here in years.

A strange restlessness was invading his spirit, but he chalked it up to being overworked and upset by having a woman in his life who wouldn't always consider his schedule. Virginia made her own rules and *he* had to do the adjusting. There was always Virginia's schedule to work around—her duties, her school and her studying, and then *maybe* they went to bed together.

It would be a hell of a lot easier to be with a woman who was always amenable to his schedule, his needs and wants. Except those women didn't light his fire—emotionally or physically—the way Virginia did.

Wilder climbed the side of the bluff, his feet steady and sure on the steps he'd traveled so often in his youth. He'd been here several times with his father.

They would get to the shallow cave and sit. Then slowly, easily, they would talk. There was no topic, no subject that couldn't be gone over and pulled apart here, and then never mentioned again. They had talked about a lot of things, but mostly Wilder's dad had listened. Wilder had learned a lot from those talks. He'd learned to voice a problem and logically work it through to a satisfying conclusion. It wasn't until he was older that Wilder realized his father had led him through the thinking process, and given him a gift—a tool—he'd use for the rest of his life.

Wilder sat on a wide, flat rock just outside the shelter of the overhang and stared across the high desert. To his right was the home he'd built ten years ago, when his father had given him the land. Wilder had been living here ever since he'd opened his first assembly line. It was a perfect home to raise a flock of kids, and someday he would.

But not now.

Right now, the idea scared the hell out of him.

He'd been an only child. Growing up, he had always wished for brothers and sisters. His parents had, too. Yet even with the oil lamp, they hadn't gotten one.

His mother never said anything, and why he was an only child was a topic his father would not discuss. From the one day they'd talked about it, Wilder hadn't believed in that damn lamp. His father had winked at the lamp story and wouldn't discuss having other children, which pointed to the fact that the fairy tales his mother wove about the piece of clay were delusional.

Especially the one that said people fell in love and lived happily ever after.

Then this little sprite of a woman comes along and thumbs her nose at his assumptions by taking an ancient, flaking clay lamp instead of the cold hard cash she needed so much. She believed when he didn't.

He heard rocks sliding and turned his head, searching the path below.

Virginia, dressed in bright green biking shorts and a sexy, little, black knit top that showed off her bare midriff, was climbing the trail.

She looked up and flashed him a bright smile when she spotted him. "Hi there," she called. "When your mom said you were headed in this direction, I couldn't wait to follow." She had almost reached him, but something she saw in his expression made her halt. "You don't mind, do you?" she asked. "If you want to be alone, I'll understand. I can see this place another time."

Seeing her, Wilder was filled with relief. She wasn't with another man, she was here in front of him. Now he could discount the very thought. He stood and held out his hand. "You're here now," he said, before realizing how ungracious it sounded. He hadn't wanted her to know what a flood of warm emotions he'd experienced, seeing her. He softened his words with a smile. "I've been wanting to show the ancient art gallery to you, anyway."

She took his hand and the last step at the same time,

and then she was standing on the ledge intimately close to him. "Art gallery?"

He nodded. "The kind I'd love to have on my wall at home, but the timing isn't right. I can't go back four or five thousand years and I don't have a limestone bluff in the living room."

Her eyes danced at the thought. "Wouldn't that have been some kind of wonderful!" She looked up at his mouth, and the words she was about to speak got caught in her throat. She swallowed hard. "It would be nice if you kissed me first," she murmured softly. "Then showed me the gallery second."

Wilder was no fool. He did as he was told, covering her mouth with his own and sipping from her sweetness. Her hand soothed every muscle she touched. The rest of him tensed in craving. When she finally pulled away, he was reluctant to end the kiss that was warming his soul.

"*You're* some kind of wonderful," he rasped, tightening his grasp on her hips, which were pressed against his.

Virginia's slow grin was delightfully impish. "Sex maniac," she declared conversationally. "Now show me your etchings."

He was grateful for her banter because it took the edge off his heightened emotions. He didn't want to delve into that territory. He'd done enough soul searching for one day.

Not letting go of her waist, Wilder led her toward the end of the shallow cave. "Here we are," he declared with a sweep of his free hand. "We're in the center of the Hunnicut Art Gallery."

She walked closer, her eyes wide with wonder. There were several drawings rendered in faded red paint. Slowly, carefully, she studied each one, reminding Wilder of how *he* had once gazed on the same drawings. Now, with Virginia by his side, he was seeing them again as if for the very first time.

"It's wonderful," she said softly.

"It is, isn't it?"

She glanced around the overhang. "And where's the cave, boss?"

"Sealed."

But she wasn't about to let it go so easily. "Where?"

He pointed toward where a bush clung to life in the dip of a large rock. "Right there."

Virginia stared. "You sealed it with a rock?"

"There's a layer of chicken wire, then concrete, then the rock. My dad sealed it after we spent almost a full day getting a spelunker out. He'd gotten himself wedged into a corner."

"When was that?"

"About fifteen years ago. This is private property and we're responsible, even for trespassers. Since the cave isn't stable, we sealed it to protect it as well as us. When the time comes for further investigation, the seal can be easily broken."

Virginia stared down at the rim of the hole. "It looks small."

"The entrance is. It widens into a large chamber with

several offshoots about thirty feet down. My dad and I explored them before he sealed it. It's fantastic, but scary." Wilder smiled at the memory. It was nice to be reminded of his youth, especially these days, when there were so many grown-up problems in his life.

"Sounds like your dad was a really neat guy," Virginia said, a touch of envy lacing her voice.

"He was. It's nice to be reminded of him."

"Do you think you'll be as good a father as he was?" Virginia asked.

Wilder felt his body freeze, then heat up. "What makes you ask?"

She looked up at him, unafraid of his closed expression. "Curiosity more than anything, I guess. I know how I feel about being a mama." She tilted her head in query. "Why? Do you feel I have designs on your genes?"

His smile felt stilted. "Of course not."

"Liar." She sat on the same rock where he'd perched earlier and stared across the river at the sand-colored bluff beyond. "I'm just asking for your opinion, since you're a man. Someday I'll be married and have a husband who wants children, too, I hope. Meanwhile, I'm collecting all the information I can get on the subject."

The image of Virginia marrying and having babies stung him like a thousand wasps. He backed away from the thought immediately and concentrated on giving her as clinical an answer as possible. "I think I'll be a great father once I'm there. But I'm not ready yet. It's a scary thing to be in charge of another human life."

Virginia had no such doubts. "I can't wait."

"What about your career?"

She gave him a look that silently questioned his sanity. "Someday a woman will be allowed to play more than one role, and her husband will be as responsible for the children as she is. They will have a partnership, not a dictatorship based on gender."

"It's a nice thought, Virginia, but I can't see the world getting there anytime soon." Thank God. She might have been married by now, if it had. "You'll just have to settle for reality instead of fairy tales. Remember, if you had chosen the money, you'd have been five hundred dollars richer, and you'd have this job to boot."

"Maybe. Maybe not. I'm not sure you would have offered me this job if I'd taken the money and run."

"Maybe, maybe not," he repeated. "We'll never know, will we?"

"No. But we do know one thing for sure. You, Wilder, are not as up on today's culture as you thought you were. You're hanging out with jaded old politicians and power brokers who are used to everyone bowing to them. They aren't representative of American men anymore."

"Everyone I meet is an anomaly, then," he retorted mildly.

"You haven't met everyone, Wilder," she said softly. "Men around the world are slowly changing, you know. They're rediscovering family, finding pride in the doing, not just the owning. They want more from life than money. They want someone who cares for them, and they're realizing they must show care in return. Surely you've seen some of that in your own world, small as it is."

It was Wilder's turn to glare at her. He wanted to believe...but it wouldn't work, didn't work that way. "You don't think much of a working man, do you?"

"I think you're a genius to build a successful company from nothing. But I also think you're lonely and you don't even know it."

He stiffened as if she'd slapped him. "Don't feel sorry for me," he retorted sharply. "I certainly don't need pity."

Virginia stood, reaching out to rest her hand on his arm. "I'm sorry."

Before he could say another word, she was walking away, carefully maneuvering down the hillside.

Wilder wanted to call her back, take her in his arms and hold her close until the heavy beating of his heart quieted.

But he didn't.

Instead, he watched her in silence and tried to convince himself that he felt lonely and unloved right now because this was the place he used to come to be close to his dad, and his dad was gone.

But so was Virginia.

LATER THAT NIGHT, Virginia dressed and left to visit friends from school who had invited her to join them for the evening. She hadn't planned on going, but after the cave episode, she realized just how enmeshed in Wilder her emotions were becoming and how much she needed a change of scenery and a new perspective.

The party was great, the company was great, but Virginia felt lonely. They were all gathered in her friend Brandon's apartment, drinking cheap wine and wondering what was next for them in the great race for career. Three women and six men were there—all different ages and races, with different interests. All were trying for something that most people took for granted you could learn as a short-order cook in a diner.

They argued, exchanged recipes, discussed temperamental chefs and where they wanted to go in life. They laughed.

And inside, Virginia prayed that Wilder would miss her this evening, that he would talk to her tomorrow at breakfast. She wished he'd grow up enough to deserve her love.

Late that night she drove home, feeling in the doldrums. Slipping into her nightgown, she sat on the bed and stared at her toes.

She'd told him what she thought, and it had scared him off. When would she learn to keep her mouth shut? All the wishes in the world wouldn't help her if she couldn't change that attribute.

When her door opened, she looked up, startled.

Wilder stood in the doorway, bare chested, midnight blue pajama bottoms slung low on his hips. "You're home," he said.

"Yes."

"I was worried."

"Thank you."

"I...we missed you at dinner."

"Sorry."

"Did you have a nice time?"

"Very. Thank you for asking."

"Is everything all right?"

She nodded. "Fine. I'm sorry if I made you uncomfortable this afternoon. I said what was on my mind when I should have filtered it first."

"No problem."

"Well..." She hesitated, not knowing quite what to say. She knew what she wanted, though. It wasn't going to happen as long as he stood in the doorway, hanging on to a doorknob as if it were a magic carpet, ready to whisk him away.

"Virginia," he began, as if finally making up his mind about speaking. "I'm not going to commit to you forever. I may never do that with anyone, I don't know. But I do know I want to be with you, for whatever time we have together."

She heard him loud and clear. He wanted a temporary commitment from her. The question was, would she be willing to settle for the now, knowing that later might never come?

Virginia smiled sadly. "You smooth-talking devil," she said softly. Then, slowly, she held out her hand to him.

Wilder accepted it. And after making sweet, tender love, he held it all through the night.

9

VIRGINIA HAD NEVER FELT so wonderful and warm and loved in all her life. Every morning she awoke to have coffee on the patio with Wilder. They talked, shared the newspaper, laughed and touched—discreetly, of course. Occasionally, his mother joined them, and the feeling of camaraderie was unchanged.

Virginia floated off to school three feet above the ground. She knew how Cinderella felt after finding her prince. The only problem was, no matter how high she felt, she knew that sooner or later she'd crash. She just hoped that when she hit bottom, Wilder would be there, too. But if he wasn't, at least she'd had this magical time with him. No one would ever be able to take these memories away from her.

Two weeks later, Wilder brought a yellow rose to the patio table. "Good morning, ladies," he said to both women, but his intense, blue-eyed gaze warmed Virginia. "Beautiful day."

"Isn't it though?" she said, peering over the top of the newspaper and loving the view of Wilder standing between the French doors and looking at her as if she was dessert and he wasn't through eating. She wanted to pinch herself awake, yet she didn't want to disturb the dream. She loved him, thought he loved her, and she was willing to pretend it was so until proven wrong.

"A rose for our personal assistant," he said, handing Virginia the flower. "I'm about to ask a favor, so I thought I'd grease the wheels a little."

"Obviously, the favor isn't from your mother," Mrs. Hunnicut observed drolly. "Or there would be two flowers."

"Sorry, Mom. But I know you'll stick around in hard times. I'm not so sure about Virginia, here."

"Really? And what hard times are we talking about, Mr. Hunnicut?" Virginia smiled widely. "Something that would go against my job description or something that would cost me money?"

"Time *is* money, Ms. Gallagher. It's your time and my money."

Her grin was impish. "A wonderful combination, I might add."

He sat down beside her, his calf touching hers. From the look he gave her, she knew he'd brushed her leg on purpose. "I'm hosting a small party in the corporate boardroom for some of our biggest distributors. I want them to have the best of everything while they're in town, and I'd like you to be in on the planning, including and especially the food. I want you at the party, too, of course."

"I'd love to help out. I'll get together with Natalie today."

Maggie came out with a wicker basket full of steaming rolls and a pot of honey butter. "When is that party, Mr. Wilder?" she asked.

"The end of next week, and I promise we won't have any houseguests this time, Maggie. They're coming in from Los Angeles and Taiwan, and we'll be putting them up at a hotel."

"I just need to know because the phone goes crazy a few days before these things. If I know what's going on, it's easier on me and my trotting legs."

"Good grief, Maggie. You make yourself sound like an old woman," Mrs. Hunnicut chastised.

"Fifty-six ain't nothin' to sneeze at," Maggie said.

"Balderdash," Mrs. Hunnicut exclaimed. "Fifty-six is nothing. Period. I'm elev..." The older woman stopped. "I'm *several* years older. You're just a baby."

"If you say so, but I swear my knees don't know it," Maggie responded. "Especially with Mr. Wilder's preferences."

"What preferences?"

Virginia tensed. She felt Wilder tensing also. It would be so embarrassing if Maggie...

"Three floors, three flights of stairs in his house design, ma'am. It keeps my heart young, but my knees old."

Laughter poured from Virginia for just a moment— she'd thought Maggie was going to comment on Wilder's sleeping arrangements, and she was mightily relieved it hadn't happened. Although she loved Wilder, she didn't want to have to explain to his mother why, more nights than not, his bed wasn't slept in.

Someday, she kept hoping, Wilder would see the futility of subterfuge and openly announce their love. That was *her* fantasy, of course—one that might never come to pass. But where there was love, there was always hope.

She glanced at Wilder through her lashes. He was drinking his coffee, but his eyes were fixed on her. He read her mind and smiled.

She prayed that smile meant what she thought it did. She prayed it meant that he was as involved and in love as she was. If only she'd thought out that last wish before making it...

When Wilder left for work, Virginia knew it was time she did the same. She had no classes today, so it was the perfect time to get hold of Natalie and get the details on the party. But there was something Virginia needed to know first. "Mrs. Hunnicut?"

"Yes, dear?"

"If you want to remake a wish, would you do the same thing you did the first time?"

The older woman looked at her over the small, wire-rimmed bifocals perched on her nose. "My dear, you can't remake a wish. That's why I said you had to be so careful in your wording. Have you already made three wishes?"

"No, but the second wish wasn't quite right," she explained uneasily. "I'd like to be more specific."

"If you do, consider it your third wish."

"Are you sure?"

"My husband took the lamp to a professor at the

University of Texas archeology school. The professor had seen one or two in the Southwest before this one was discovered. According to the legend my husband was told—confirmed by the pictographs on the cave wall—those are the rules."

Virginia's hope flickered. "Well, thanks anyway," she said.

Mrs. Hunnicut stopped the hope from dying. "My dear, if you want money, you can always make your three wishes and then sell the lamp. I'm sure any respectable museum would take it off your hands for a tidy sum. But if you don't need the money, your best avenue is to find some other deserving woman and pass it on. You do far more good by giving someone else a chance at her dreams."

"Does it necessarily have to go to a woman?"

Wilder's mother chuckled. "No, not really. But it does seem to me that even in this day and age we woman need more divine help than any mortal man."

"I'm almost afraid to make that third wish," Virginia admitted. "What if I need it later?"

"I understand, my dear. I felt the same way, hoping I didn't have to use it." Mrs. Hunnicut stared out over the creek, her gaze focused on the past instead of the present. "But it wasn't to be. I needed it for my husband and my family, and I was so glad I hadn't made other wishes, frivolous wishes compared to the need to protect the people you love."

How true, Virginia thought, walking back into the library to begin the day's work. The prospect of being so

closely involved with Wilder planning this party gave
her hope. Finally she could show him *everything* she
was. She could show him that Virginia Gallagher was
socially acceptable, socially at ease. She hoped.

Just in case, she called Natalie and left a message on
her voice mail. "Nat? Virginia. Do you have any tips on
etiquette for this upcoming party?"

THE WEEK SPED BY. Natalie helped in so many ways that
occasionally Virginia felt like a Siamese twin—the one
who wasn't leading. To say Wilder's assistant was organized was misleading. She was a walking computer.
She remembered every little fact. Natalie was dyna-
mite, and Virginia wanted to be just like her, but
couldn't, and finally in a weak moment she admitted it.

"I finally find my idol," she said, "and it's too late."

"Who and why?" Natalie asked.

"*You*. And I'm hell-bent on another career that re-
quires its own level of organization, but nothing compared to this."

Natalie gave her a quick, commiserating grin, then
went back to the papers in front of her, murmuring,
"I'd say split-second timing is everything in cooking. I
can afford to be a little more lax than that."

Virginia laughed. The woman had no idea she was a
dynamo, any more than she was aware of her fresh
beauty. Amazing.

Natalie was perfect for Wilder, so Virginia didn't ask
any more about her. She wasn't fool enough to show
his heart the way to another woman. In fact, Virginia

was amazed that he appeared so oblivious of Natalie; he saw her all day long. Yet almost every night he spent with Virginia. He made love to her as if she were his source of energy. As if...as if he loved her. He was now in the habit of sleeping in her bed until a little after four, when he would get up and run three or four miles. There was no doubt in Virginia's mind that she loved him, but she wasn't so in love that she'd take up running!

She prayed every morning that she'd made the right decision in asking for someone to love her. She didn't want Wilder's love to be prompted by an old clay lamp. She wanted his love to be based on his true feelings and needs for her.

ON THE NIGHT OF THE PARTY Virginia felt as if this was her graduation and she was the valedictorian. Butterflies fluttered in her stomach, sweat was popping out on her brow and she knew she'd taken a chance when she'd spent the last two days teaching a catering company how to make her three specialty hors d'ouvres. Not the best way to make her debut.

She would take all the flack if the food wasn't right for this grouping. Natalie had given her free rein and then stayed out of the way completely. She hadn't even checked on Virginia's choice of caterers or staff. There was no one but Virginia to blame if things went wrong.

She splurged and bought a snappy tobacco brown dress from a secondhand store that took in the castaways of the affluent. Even coming from there, a first-

class piece cost an arm and a leg, but Virginia knew she
would always get her money's worth from quality.

She'd brought her new dress with her to the office so
she wouldn't have to waste time driving back and
forth. She blamed Wilder for that. He was so time con-
scious that she was getting that way, too. Organization,
he said. That was the key.

Uh-huh. Sure.

She changed in the corporate offices' ladies' room.
Pausing to look in the mirror, Virginia wondered if
that was really her gazing back. If it was, she was better
looking than she'd ever been.

For once, her hair was doing what it was supposed
to do. It was pulled back softly from her face and
curled behind her ears.... The makeup Natalie had
helped her with was just right: a peach blush, a light
dusting of matt powder, mascara and tobacco-toned
eye shadow following the contour of her lids. Virginia
was amazed. She hadn't known a few cosmetics could
make such a difference.

"Okay, woman," she told her image. "Get out there
and dazzle 'em with your sophistication." Virginia
took one more deep breath and stepped through the
outer door.

She saw Natalie and Wilder right away, in the foyer
leading to the elevators, greeting guests as they arrived. Natalie seemed so competent, so easy with the
whole enterprise. Virginia wished that her emotions
were as controlled.

She at least knew her role in this soiree.

She headed directly toward the small kitchen/serving area behind the boardroom. Three women scurried around, arranging platters, pouring sauces and lining up clean glasses for the eight young waiters who were carrying trays.

The head of catering—an older woman who knew her stuff, if her resumé was anything to go by—smiled in Virginia's direction. "How's it going out there?"

"Looks like most of the guests are here. Is everything going okay in here?"

"Don't have more than the usual problems. A bowl broke, several strawberries in the bottom of the carton were rotten." She wiped a strand of hair off her forehead with her arm. "Last time I use *that* market."

"Champagne tray coming through," called one of the young waiters as he charged by with a precarious burden balanced on a tray.

Virginia flattened herself against the counter to let him pass, then spied his tray and stopped him. "Wait. What are you doing with plastic glasses?"

"Only half of them are plastic. We were running low on glass and they were in the cupboard, so I thought I'd use them instead of waiting for the glass ones to be washed."

"No. We use nothing but glass." Virginia insisted. "If the glasses aren't ready, wash them yourself." She paused, looking him over. "And this isn't feeding time at the zoo. Slow down. Your attitude's going to give them indigestion."

She received a heavy sigh and dirty look from the

waiter, but he did what he was told. That's all she wanted.

When Virginia walked out to check on the buffet table she was pleased with everything. She'd worked all afternoon to insure a wonderful presentation. And it was.

A deep voice from behind her whispered in her ear, "Everything looks great. Giving yourself a pat on the back yet?"

"Not yet, Wilder, but I will soon," she promised softly, turning to confront him. He looked so very handsome it took her breath away. He was freshly shaved and she was close enough to catch the scent of his shaving lotion. She breathed in deeply. It was fast becoming her favorite scent. He was wearing a white tuxedo—obviously hand tailored—that showed off his broad shoulders and trim hips to perfection.

"Have I passed the examination?" he teased.

"You get an *A* just because you know how to tie one of those," she said. "It looks just as good as a clip-on."

"Gee whiz, that's exactly what I was striving for, ma'am."

"You've achieved your goal, then." She said beneficently, glancing over his shoulder toward a small group of people clustered in the entryway. With relief, she spotted Natalie heading in that direction with a waiter. She looked back up at Wilder, who was studying her with interest. "But you could have bought a ready-made clip-on and saved yourself the effort."

"What a sweet child. And your mother taught you

your manners?" he said dryly, but the look he gave her was far more heated and intimate than his tone of voice.

Her eyes widened innocently. "Too direct and to the point?"

"Yes." He sighed. "But at least I always know where I stand." His gaze ran up and down her body and appreciation shone in his eyes. "I'll be direct, too. I didn't think it was possible for you to look any better than when you wear that white, silky thing. But I was wrong. You look fantastic."

"Thank you," she managed to say. "So do you."

"So do I what?" he prompted.

"Look fantastic."

"I thought you'd never say it. Now. How do you like my tie?"

"It's fantastic. Everything about you is fantastic."

"Fantastic," said a man Virginia didn't know. He clasped Wilder's shoulder and added, "An underrated word, don't you think?"

Wilder's mouth turned up in a grin. "It's about time you got here. You were supposed to be here to greet Mr. Tito."

"I did greet Mr. Tito, just a few minutes after you did the deed." His eyes turned toward Virginia, lighting up in appreciation. "Fantastic."

Both Virginia and Wilder burst out laughing.

"Thank you," she finally said, holding out her hand. "I'm Virginia Gallagher."

"And I'm Pete Major. Your boss's best friend," he

said, stepping a little closer as if to edge Wilder out of the picture. "He mentioned you, but I had no idea you were so pretty. My old pal Wilder must have had his head buried in his computer not to mention how brilliant a star in his sky you were."

Pete's lighthearted banter sat well with the mischievous look in his eyes. He wasn't leering, but he was getting his point across. "Well, thank you," Virginia said. "He hadn't mentioned it to me, either, so we're even."

Pete didn't even glance at Wilder. "Really!" he said. "He ought to be ashamed of himself. And since I know his mother, I also know it's not her fault. She tried her best to teach him manners, but some boys never learn."

Virginia withdrew her hand slowly, trying not to appear too interested. Wilder looked as if he'd eaten thunder. "She's a dear, isn't she?"

"And she's sitting over by the couch, waiting for you to say hello," Wilder said.

Virginia's gaze darted in his direction. "So she is." She murmured. "Please excuse me, won't you, Mr. Major? Duty, although pleasant, calls."

He bowed his sandy-blond head. "I'm at your service as soon as you're free. Promise me a dance, Virginia, and I'll be in heaven."

Her eyes widened. "Dance?" Three musicians sat in the corner playing classical music. There was a flute, a violin and a cello.

"Of course, haven't you heard? Mozart is all the rage."

She couldn't help it; her laughter burst forth. His impish humor was irresistible. "I'll keep my dance card open," she promised.

"Pete, I think Ms. Gallagher needs to get on with her work," Wilder catered through gritted teeth.

Surprised, Virginia looked up at him. Was he saying that their's was no more than a business relationship? Was he denying everything they meant to each other?

"Well, Wilder, old pal." There was a hint of a challenge in Pete Major's tone, but his smile seemed genuine. "I'd say that your guest list is overloaded with beautiful women, so if you don't mind, I'll just walk Ms. Gallagher over so I can keep her company a little longer, and pay my respects to your mom."

"I wanted to introduce you to Representative Williams," Wilder said.

"And you will. Later, pal."

Pete took Virginia's arm and steered her directly across the room, lifting a glass of champagne off a tray and handing it to her as they went.

"Have you been friends long?" Virginia asked, sipping from the delicate flute.

"Since sixth grade." Pete snagged a glass from a passing waiter for himself. "Long enough to know when Wilder's upset. Like now."

"Now? He has no reason to be."

"No, he doesn't." Pete seemed easy with himself and with her. "But it will do him good to stew. Everything comes easy to Wilder. Especially women. It's time he went through a little of the struggle *mortal* men face."

"And your taking me away will do that?"

"It will if he's as smart as I think he is."

"And what makes you think he's interested to begin with?"

"I've known him since sixth grade, remember?"

"And are you friend or foe?"

"Friend."

They reached Mrs. Hunnicut's side and Pete leaned down to kiss her cheek. "How's my favorite mom?" he asked.

"Pete! I'm so glad you came. How's San Antonio treating you?"

"Pretty well, but not well enough to keep me there for very long. Austin's only an hour away, but it might as well be another world."

"You're speeding again," Mrs. Hunnicut admonished. "We're a sedate, legal two hours away."

Pete sat on the edge of the marshmallow leather couch and made himself comfortable. "How 'bout you give and I give and we call it an hour and a half."

"Excuse me," Virginia murmured. "I need to check on the food." She left them deep in conversation and wandered around until she found Wilder talking to a group of men who had just walked in. He was introducing them to a cluster of people already standing by the bar. Apparently he was too busy with his guests to acknowledge her presence.

She went to check on the kitchen again, telling herself it didn't matter that Wilder hadn't acknowledged they were a couple, at least for the time being. She didn't want that to matter because she didn't want to admit how much it hurt....

OUT OF THE CORNER of his eye, Wilder watched Virginia walk through the doors, heading toward the kitchen. He wanted to kick himself for acting the way he had. He should have just told Pete to lay off. All it would have taken was a few words. But Wilder had missed the boat, and when Pete was in one of his moods, he could charm the birds out of the trees. He was obviously in one of those moods tonight.

When Virginia reappeared, Wilder watched her walk across the room. She discreetly monitored one of the waiters serving hors d'oeuvres while checking on the buffet table. She kept an eye on the waiter as he carried a tray of her creations over to Wilder's group.

Everyone was offered, and most took tiny spring rolls, Virginia had prepared Southwestern style—miniature flour tortillas stuffed with delicious chicken and sauce. Wilder ate his in one bite. One of his guests called the waiter back for seconds.

Wilder felt such pride in her. He wanted to tell everyone she was his. He wanted to hear how lucky he was to have such a talented, beautiful woman in his life. But he couldn't find the nerve to admit publically that his relationship with Virginia was more than skin-deep. He didn't want to face that. Not yet. Not when she was hell-bent on leaving, and he would be standing alone, soon enough, left holding an empty bag.

Funny. He could speak up loudly in business when

others couldn't find a voice, make decisions that others feared to make, demand better parts, service, products. But when it came to his personal life, he couldn't express his pride, his wants, his needs.

Better that no one knew how deeply and strongly he felt about Virginia. This way no one would pity him later, when she was gone.

PETE KEPT VIRGINIA laughing all through the evening. Everywhere she turned, he was at her elbow or just behind her with his rapier-sharp wit. He had a comment to make about anything and everything.

"See that young guy over there?"

Virginia nodded.

"He's the largest manufacturer of a specific computer chip in Taiwan."

"He must be very wealthy," she said.

"He is, but he's still having a hard time saying no to his mother's choice of a bride."

"Really?"

Pete nodded sadly. "She chose a girl so plain she could stop a spotted carp from swimming downstream. But the young lady has money and is willing to allow Mom to rule."

Virginia tried not to laugh. "Why does he let his mother influence him at all?" she asked.

"Because she's his largest stockholder."

Virginia finally gave in to laughter. "No!"

Pete never cracked his deadpan face. "Honest. She threatened to vote him out of his own company."

Virginia retained her composure, but just barely.

From the corner of her eye, she saw Wilder's mother motioning to her, and she excused herself.

"I just wanted to tell you that everyone is raving about your little creations," Mrs. Hunnicut said. "Everyone including your boss. Wilder's so puffed up you'd think he'd invented the hors d'oeuvre."

"Are they good enough to get me a job somewhere across the country?" Virginia asked, proud of her accomplishment yet unwilling to make too big a deal out of it. She didn't know what—perhaps modesty, perhaps superstition—kept her from claiming the praise.

"My dear, they're good enough to get you far, far away from Wilder, if that's your wish."

Virginia began to protest: "I didn't mean..."

But the older woman patted her hand. "I know, but that's what it all boils down to, *doesn't* it?"

Virginia didn't know what to say. Succeeding as a chef had been her dream for so long, and yet now that she was close to realizing that dream, she was hanging back.

Achieving her goal meant leaving the man she loved. And the man she loved didn't even know it.

How ironic. She was pining away for a guy who didn't seem to have an ounce of feeling for her unless she was in his bed.

10

VIRGINIA SNUGGLED into Wilder's lightly furred chest, loving the strength of his arms encircling and holding her. Still asleep, he lightly kissed the top of her head. She felt secure and treasured.

They'd come home from the party a little past midnight, and Wilder had been by her side all night. He'd been funny and loving and tender and caring. He'd made love to her as if she were a movie goddess, then protectively tucked her near his heart and promptly fell asleep.

Virginia slept, too, only to dream about the two of them. Throughout the long night, she woke occasionally to ensure that he was still holding her. Her dreams were fuzzy, hazy wonders that left her feeling soft and feminine and content with the world—no matter what. Her mother, Irish wonder that she was, had always sworn that bad dreams were fears you didn't want to face and good dreams were wishes you were afraid to acknowledge. Leave it to the Irish, Virginia thought, to confuse good and bad.

She allowed her hand to run the length of Wilder's side and feel the lean, strong manliness of him.

The next thing she knew, sunlight was registering on her groggy brain and her eyes popped open.

Trying not to disturb Wilder, she peeked over his shoulder at the clock radio behind him. Darn! Just as she thought. Even if she hurried, really hurried, she'd be half an hour late for class. This was the last week of classes and each day featured a different guest chef from somewhere around the country. She didn't want to miss a single minute. Who knew? Today might just be the one when a visiting chef offered her patronage.

She wiggled out of the sheets and practically sprinted to the bathroom. Her flight was cut short only by Wilder's voice.

"Hey! Come back to bed, darlin'," he cajoled, his tone husky and sensuous. He rolled over and propped his head up on one strong arm. The warm light in his eyes was almost enough to make her slow down. Almost, but not quite.

"Fame and fortune awaits. I have class in less than an hour."

"Can't you skip it for a day?"

She raised one eyebrow. "Are you staying home from work?"

"Well..." He frowned. "For an hour or so."

She walked toward the bathroom door, trying not to let him see the hurt on her face. "I don't have an hour or so to spare. If I wait, the class will be in full swing. It's either all or nothing, Wilder, so I guess it's nothing."

"What's the harm..."

She looked over her shoulder. Anger had burned away her hurt, and she let the anger show. She couldn't believe he was so dense that he didn't see he was diminishing her duties while implying his were too important to give up. "Please don't. It's beneath you."

With quiet determination, she closed the door between them and turned on the shower. By the time she stepped out of the bathroom again he was gone.

"You could have made the bed, Wilder," she muttered angrily, using that emotion as a barrier to the intense hurt. Quickly she smoothed the sheets and shook out the comforter. Slipping into a pair of jeans she grabbed a T-shirt that had seen better days, and pulled it on. When she reached school, she'd be downing a smock apron that looked much like a lab coat, and no one would know just how sloppy she looked underneath.

She barely made it to class on time. A chef from one of the most chic spas in Dallas was already preparing a dinner fit for a slim king when she walked in. Charlie Feather's disapproving gaze lit on her for a long moment before he turned his attention to the demonstration. Not willing to carry all the blame, she silently cursed Wilder.

She loved him, and that was reason enough to hate his attitude. She cursed him all day.

Finally, the day was done. As she was washing her hands, Charlie came up behind her. "If you say you'll be here, be here. I wanted to introduce you to Chef Pierce before this started."

She felt disappointment take hold in the pit of her stomach. "Can't I meet him now, Charlie?"

"Too late." Charlie nodded toward the back door. "He's got a plane to catch. He begged off early and I couldn't do anything about it. Not even singing your praises would stop his plane from leaving on time."

Staring over his shoulder, Virginia saw Chef Pierce being hustled out by a young woman in a chauffeur's uniform. He definitely looked as if he was in a hurry. Virginia dried her hands, then turned toward her mentor. "I'm sorry," she said "I slept late. I helped at a party last night and it wore me out."

"Get your priorities squared away, princess," Charlie said, not unkindly, "or it won't matter how good you are, you won't reach your goal."

He walked away, leaving Virginia feeling depressed and guilty. She'd worked so hard to get ahead in this school, succeeding where others hadn't. But she'd goofed. Charlie was right. She had to make up her mind what was important to her and keep that goal in sight.

Part of her laughed at that thought; until Wilder came on the scene, she'd known what was important. Now everything revolved around him—all her hopes and wishes....

Her wishes!

This whole thing had started with wishes.

She'd wished herself into this mess and now she'd goofed on her career—the one thing she'd wanted more than anything else in the world, until she'd met Wilder.

Still angry and frustrated, Virginia headed back to the house on Lick Creek. She'd created this mess out of her own choices. She'd gotten into an impossible situation with Wilder all by herself, without any help. But now it was time to turn the tide. She had to face the fact that he didn't love her, never would—her career was all she could be certain of.

If that was the case, her career had to be the most important thing in her life. She had to follow through with action that would keep her career goals in sight. That thought spawned a sense of urgency. Virginia knew she had to get on as she meant to go on. And she had to do it now.

When she reached Wilder's house, she parked and ran inside. Mrs. Hunnicut was in the living room, on a rocker by the French doors, working a small patch of quilt. "You're home early," she commented brightly. "How nice. Any particular reason?"

Virginia perched on the couch and took a deep breath. "Yes. I graduate next Thursday, and I'd like to invite you and Mr. Hunnicut and Pete Major to the graduate dinner."

The older woman put down her sewing and clasped her hands in her lap. "I can't speak for my son, Virginia, or for his upstart best friend, but I would be honored to attend. What time?"

Virginia gave her the details, then stared down at her hands for a moment.

"You can talk to me," Mrs. Hunnicut said softly.

It was all the encouragement Virginia needed. "I'm giving my notice," she said. "I'll be leaving the day after the graduation dinner."

Mrs. Hunnicut gave a heavy sigh. "I wish things had worked out differently. I had such high hopes...." Her soft voice faded away, leaving sadness hanging in the air.

Virginia didn't know if the older woman realized what she'd said or how things had "worked out" with Wilder, but she knew the heartbreak of her own topsy-turvy emotions, and she echoed the other woman's sigh. "So did I." She pasted a smile on her lips. "But all good things must come to an end. And it looks like this week will end it."

"If you say so, my dear." Mrs. Hunnicut made a few more neat stitches in the quilted material. "Have you mentioned this to my son yet?"

"Not yet," Virginia replied, "but I will."

"He'll be disappointed. I have a feeling he thought you might want to stay for a while, perhaps work for a restaurant here in town."

"Yes, well..." Virginia paused. Wilder had never hinted that thought to her. She stood, saying, "It wasn't to be. But I won't forget your kindness soon, Mrs. Hunnicut. You've helped me reach my goal, and I can't thank you enough for that."

"I understand. You must follow your path. I was just hoping, as was Wilder, that you would find the opportunity to stay." Wise gray eyes stared at Virginia as if she could see straight through to her soul. "Are you sure leaving is what you want to do?."

Virginia swallowed the lump in her throat and forced back the tears that threatened to fall. "Yes," she said.

Without another word, she quickly left the room. If she was going to cry, she was going to do so in the privacy of her own bed.

As she stretched out and the tears began to fall, she realized that this wasn't even her bedroom. With the exception of the first month, she'd shared this room with Wilder. His scent was on the coverlet, damn him!

Damn her wishes!

WILDER KNEW HE'D DONE badly by Virginia. All through his morning meeting with Natalie, throughout the board meeting and the reception with the East Coast distributors, he'd thought of her. He'd done wrong. Virginia had been right to be angry this morning. He'd negated her work while elevating his own. He'd seen it in her look, in her stance. Heard it in her words.

And he'd felt like a heel. What the hell had gotten into him that he'd demand she drop everything for him and his whims? If a woman had tried that on him, he would have dropped her like a hot coal, never looking back and secure in the knowledge that she must have been a bitch to have asked that of him.

What did that make him?

Ever since Virginia had come into his life, everything

had turned upside down. He didn't even know who he was anymore. And if the glimpse of himself he'd caught this morning was any indication of how others saw him, he didn't think he wanted to know himself.

He definitely owed Virginia an apology, but thinking about it and doing it were two different things. Instead of going home after work, he met Pete for a drink, hiding instead of facing the music immediately.

"Man, this was a day from hell," Pete said after the waitress had delivered their beer to the booth. They were in a trendy little bar just off Sixth Street, and the place was filled with men in white shirts and ties, suit coats abandoned on the seat beside them. From the look of the crowd, it had been a tough day for everyone.

"What happened?"

"My report wasn't delivered from the printing department on time, so I wasn't as well versed on the material as I should have been. The new congressman from San Antonio decided to see if he could tear me apart in public." Pete took another sip of his brew. "The usual working day on Capitol Hill." Wilder felt his friend's eyes bore into him. "What about you?"

"The little shop of horrors is shaping up. Slowly," Wilder replied.

"And because it's shaping up you decided to have a beer in a local pub with your closemouthed buddy instead of dining in some swank restaurant or going home to one of the sweetest little gals to come along in a long time?" Pete's eyebrows rose in query, but he answered the question himself. "I think not."

Wilder looked at his beer. "It's true."

Pete wasn't about to give up. Damn guy was like a cat with yarn. Wilder knew his friend would keep hitting at him until he got a straight answer.

As if on cue, Pete said, "I repeat—what about you?"

"Work. Work is about me. I'm in the middle of a budget fight and it's hell."

"It always is." Pete relaxed in his seat. "I wish my budget fights were like yours. You don't run out of money, you're just not sure whether you want to put it into research, development, publicity and promotion or more sales staff. Or should you give it to the poor or vote the board of directors a bonus? Gee, I wonder what to do?"

Wilder harrumphed. "Oversimplification, buddy. My battles are just as bloody as yours any day. Sometimes more so."

"Then it's got to be your personal life. Greta giving you a problem? I noticed she wasn't at the cocktail party."

"No, no problem." Hell, he hadn't seen her in over three months. Not since Virginia had entered the picture. "What about you?"

"Well, I won't have a problem if I can get your new little assistant to pay attention to me." Pete's grin was wide. "She's a real looker *and* she's got a smart head on her shoulders. What a combination!"

Alarm bells went off in Wilder's brain, clanging so

loudly he barely heard the din of the bar. He couldn't have heard right. He couldn't have.... "Virginia?"

"Of course, Virginia. You didn't notice that I flipped over her?"

It took all the restraint Wilder had to not grit his teeth. "No, I guess I didn't."

"And I think she likes me, too."

If she was two-timing him, he'd... He'd what? Be a bigger fool than he'd already shown himself to be? "What makes you think she likes you?"

"She was open and receptive. She smiles at me a lot. And she seemed to like my sense of humor." Pete looked abashed. "And you know how many women think my humor is weird. But not little Virginia."

"Sounds more like she was acting the good hostess." Wilder took another gulp of beer.

"And *that* sounds more like a dog in a manger," Pete retorted dryly.

That hit a nerve. "That's not true. I just don't think Virginia was giving you a come-on. Doing those things is her way of being friendly, that's all."

"And this afternoon," Pete said with a smug smile on his face, "she called and left word with my secretary that she wanted me at her graduation this Thursday."

The air was knocked out of Wilder's lungs and he felt something akin to panic. His vocal cords seized up. He stalled for time by motioning to the waitress for another round of beer. He'd forgotten Virginia was due to graduate. He'd forgotten that time was running out, and he had treated her as if she was hired help he just so happened to sleep with, make love to, laugh with, live with. He'd forgotten so damn much and never bothered to refresh his memory by asking her about her work. In fact, he'd made a concerted effort not to ask. He hadn't wanted to know any more about it, because asking would mean he cared. And God forbid Virginia should think that! He was the rich and powerful Wilder Hunnicut, and she was just a young, lonely, wannabe chef. Man, had he messed up. Bigtime.

When he could swallow again, he asked the question uppermost on his mind. "And what did you say?"

"I couldn't get back to her. By the time I called, she was gone, so I just left a message at your house saying I would be delighted to attend and to return my call and let me know the particulars."

The waitress delivered two more beers and Wilder paid for the round.

"But you must know the time and place," Pete said. "Why don't you tell me?"

"Sorry to disappoint you, but I don't know a damn thing. I haven't seen her for two days. You'll have to get it from the horse's mouth."

"Don't sound so bitter, old man. You had your chance and you chose not to take it. Now it's my turn to see if the lovely lady wants to have me worship at her feet."

"Don't get too poetic, Pete. Start as you mean to go on or you'll never make a woman happy."

"Right," his friend snorted. "Like you, I suppose,

who decided that all women need to be treated like cattle, so they'll know they're not important right off the bat. Thanks, but I'll take my chances my way. At least I'm willing to admit I've got flaws, but I might learn to get better." Pete looked at him sharply. "*You* act as if this is as good as you're going to get and you might get a hell of a lot worse."

Wilder winced at that. "You don't know that."

"I've been your friend for more years than I care to admit, and many of your women have cried on my shoulder because of you. I have a fairly good idea about how you treat the fair sex."

Anger flooded Wilder. It was anger aimed at himself. How could he be so good in business and so bad in love? "You don't know a damn thing, buddy. You just think you do." Wilder stood and threw down a tip. "I've got to get back home. I promised Mom. I'd help her get ready to go home tonight."

Pete looked more than a little bewildered. "Hey, man, I'm sorry if I hurt your feelings. I didn't know you had a sore spot in that area." He stood, too, stretching out his hand.

It took everything Wilder had to shake it, but he did. He clasped Pete's hand for all of a second, then dropped it.

They'd had conversations along this line before, but Wilder had never taken umbrage in the past. But no matter how much he tried, he couldn't let go of his anger. "Talk to you later," he said tersely, then left the bar without a backward glance.

Sammy was outside with the van, patiently waiting as usual.

All the way home, Wilder attempted to get his emotions under control. Turning on his computer, he forced himself to concentrate on problems that had nothing to do with one little imp of a chef. By the time they reached the house, he could at least breathe without sounding like a freight train huffing into the station.

His mother sat by the French doors, her sewing in her lap and the saddest expression he'd seen in years on her face. He stopped, staring at the woman who had raised him so well. She'd given much to him and his father, while maintaining her own identity, which wasn't an easy feat. Sometimes he'd resented the fact that she'd kept something for herself. He'd wanted her to give him her all. But he'd been young then, and his ideas about life, living and women hadn't been formed with reality and rightness in mind. Things were different now. Now he knew. His mother had given him even more because she had refused to give in to the demand to blend and disappear into a life that wasn't her own. Had she put her life aside for theirs, she would have had no life at all, and he would have had to care for her emotionally as well as physically now.

Instead, his mother had a strong personality and a strong voice; she had definite interests and good friends. In short, she was her own interesting, fun and loving person. He was damn lucky she was still in his life.

Swallowing the lump in his throat, Wilder entered the room. "Are you all right?" he asked softly, bending down to place a light kiss on her soft, wrinkled cheek. "What's bothering you?"

She turned, smiling at her son. "I'm glad you're home. I miss you," she said slowly. She looked back out at the creek below. "I was just thinking how much of my life was spent in this area. Everywhere I turn, lovely memories assault me. Your father. You. Dreams." She looked back at him, that same sad look still in her eyes. "Even the lamp."

Wilder didn't broach that subject, this wasn't the time. "I have a few of those memories myself," he answered. "Most of them are of the family—the times we've picnicked or swam or just talked on the banks of the creek."

His mother nodded. "So many memories. I even remember the fun you had building this home." She gazed at her son again. "I had such high hopes of seeing my grandchildren play here and..." She gave a sigh. "Oh, well."

"Don't pull the guilt trip, Mom."

Her eyes widened. "Is it working?"

"If I had a potential bride, I'd marry her on the spot. Just for you," he teased.

She cupped his cheek with her hand. "What a good son. I knew that. I just wish..." She gave her head a little shake. "I want you happy before I go. I know it's a selfish thing, but that's the way it is with mothers. Today is one of those days where I chose to look back on my life and see where I've been. I've had wonderful times, Wilder, but most of them didn't begin for me until I met and married your father. *That* was the beginning of life for me. I know the difference between being single and married, my dear. And being with someone you love and trust, who loves and trusts you in return, is one of the two greatest wonders of the world. The second is when you have a child and he or she grows up to be all you wished for."

"Are you saying you're proud of me?"

"I'm saying that, and a hundred things more, my darling. Even though your father was my love, without you in my life I wouldn't have been complete. But I didn't know that until after you were born."

"And I won't know that, either, until I marry and have a child. Is that what you're saying?"

"Exactly."

"Anyone in mind?" he teased, trying to lighten his mother's mood, pretending to himself that Virginia didn't fit the bill as wife and mother. She couldn't; she had her own career, her own life, and none of that was set here on Lick Creek. "I'll try to remember to forget about being a success in business. My wife and I will live on love."

"Don't be silly," his mother ordered, dropping her hand limply to her lap. "No one can live without other things. We can all do without love, laughter, money. But it's called survival, not living. I want you to live. Happily. Not like this the rest of your life."

"This?"

"Empty. Ungiving."

Unwilling to hear any more, Wilder stood. "I think that's an exaggeration, don't you?"

His mother's voice was firm, regaining its usual strength. "Not at all. And you're just a babe in the woods—I'm the experienced one. The trouble is, you think you know it all, you whippersnapper. I know better."

"I'll keep that in mind," Wilder said, heading upstairs toward his bedroom.

"Virginia's leaving this weekend," his mother called to his retreating back.

"So I heard," he stated, not missing a step. "We'll all miss her."

"Some more than others," his mother called.

Wilder knew what the answer to that was, but he refused to admit it. Instead, he took refuge in his automatic reaction—no woman, not even his mother, was going to box him into a relationship when he wasn't ready.

Just the thought of marriage was enough to fill him with fear. No man or woman would ever regulate his comings and goings, tell him when to sneeze and when to eat. No one would tell him what to do. He'd always felt that way. He was too accustomed to calling the shots for himself and others. He wasn't about to change now, he swore—but not as forcefully as usual.

11

FOR CHEFS, graduation night was a test for which there was no equal. Students put together a dinner for their families, peers and the master chef's guests. Each graduate was in charge of a particular part of the meal, and it had to be his or her own original concoction. Virginia had earned the entrée—she could choose and create the heart of the meal. Only Charlie Feather could override her decisions.

Late at night and early in the morning in Wilder's kitchen, she worked on various ideas and presentations. When both Maggie and Mrs. Hunnicut rolled their eyes after tasting her sea bass with almond pesto, she finally felt satisfaction.

That night, a crew of helpers in the cooking-school kitchen began the preparation. Virginia didn't know if Wilder would show up or not. She hadn't seen him in the past three days. Two nights he'd been called out of town, and one night she'd met with friends to celebrate the end of classes. She thought both she and Wilder were purposely avoiding a confrontation. She didn't want to confront him with the fact that she loved him, and she was sure he didn't want to admit just how little he cared. The man had some conscience, she had to admit.

But hope sprang eternal, so Virginia kept glancing through the swinging doors as the guests entered and were seated in the luxurious surroundings of a small restaurant setting. Her stomach was filled with butterflies when she saw Mrs. Hunnicut walk in on the arms of Pete and Wilder. Sadie was already assigned to a smoking table in the far corner. The Hunnicut party was seated closer to the large double doors at the side of the room.

Lisa, who was in charge of dessert, looked over Virginia's shoulder, eyes wide. "Wow, Wilder Hunnicut really came!" she whispered. "You've got to be the belle of the ball tonight Virginia. You've got the entrée, two members of the audience—owners of primo restaurants in Dallas—are interested in you and one of your guests is the most eligible, sought-after, successful businessmen on the North American continent!"

"And I'm a nervous wreck." Virginia was so scared she couldn't take a deep breath. She wished she hadn't been so creative with the fish. Not only was her job on the line, so was her self-esteem. Charlie had said her dish was perfect, but what did he know? She was cooking for a hundred people, for heaven's sake! Not *everyone* would like it!

Doubts assailed her on every front.

"Stop gawking and get it rolling," Charlie called from across the kitchen. He looked as uptight as Virginia felt.

Lisa shrugged. "Guess it's show time," she muttered before going back to the pastry table. "Break a leg."

"Same to you," Virginia murmured absently. With one more glance at Wilder's stern face, she turned and went back to work. Guests had menus offering a choice of three entrées and she'd be getting the orders any moment now.

She worried all through preparations about why Wilder was looking so disgruntled. Had something happened at work? Finally she forced herself to stop thinking of him. This was a test, not a drooling session over a man who obviously didn't feel the same way about her.

Virginia sighed. She knew Pete was interested— very interested—in her. And he was a nice guy who would make a wonderful partner and helpmate. He had a remarkable sense of humor and would probably make a great father. If the legend of the lamp was real, then Pete had probably been sent in answer to her wish. But if that was the case, why didn't she love him back?

The orders began coming in and the frantic hurry of preparing began in earnest. There was no time to think of the man who had shared her bed and her heart.

"LOVE A WOMAN with a career," Pete recommended. "It usually means she's intelligent and quick and can cope with anything."

"If that was the case, Pete, she'd be better off with the one job men can't quite seem to get a handle on until midway through the process—child rearing." Mrs. Hunnicut's eyes gleamed with merriment.

"My sentiments exactly." Pete's grin answered her own. "And all you have to do is convince her to stay home. Then everybody's got the best of both worlds."

"You're both wrong," Wilder stated disgustedly. "Women today don't want to give up the goals they've set for themselves. They want it all."

"And you don't?" his mother asked.

"Yes, but the company is my life. In a sense, I created it and gave birth to it. It's the focus of my life," Wilder stated, knowing just how lame that sounded. "I don't have time to be Mr. Mom."

"Balderdash," his mother spat. "You're spoiled and you want it both ways. You two aren't that different from the men of my generation. You want to be able to have a woman at your beck and call, but you'd like her to leave you alone while you go about your own, 'more important' business." Her wrinkled face showed her disappointment in both men, but her eyes zeroed in on her son. "No wonder women are finding boy-toys. At least there are no unreasonable demands, and you don't have to wait on them. If I was younger I'd show you little chauvinists how the cow ate the cabbage!"

Pete looked stunned, but Wilder wasn't surprised. Most of the time he loved his mother's sharp wit and outspoken ways, and the part of her that liked to shock. But not now. Not while he was struggling with the problem of losing Virginia.

After taking a deep breath to ease some of the tension, he winked at Pete. "All this from a woman who fantasizes about magic lamps," he said. "I'd worry about priorities. Besides, you're my mother, you're supposed to support me in my search for the perfect woman."

"Humph," his mother said. "Watch out, Wilder. Because if you find the perfect woman, she certainly won't want you. She'll probably be searching for the perfect man."

Pete and Wilder laughed, but an itchy feeling rode up Wilder's spine. "Aren't you supposed to be on my side, Mom?"

"I am, my wonderful son," she said softly. "But it's lonely there, you're not on your side with me. Don't shoot yourself in the foot too many times or people will think that limp is permanent."

Wilder and his mother were both delighted by the fish when it was served. Pete had ordered the shredded pork.

"Isn't she clever?" Mrs. Hunnicut enthused. "This is even tastier than the version that made me fall in love with this recipe."

"You've had it before?" Wilder asked.

"Virginia practiced on Maggie and me several times," she said. "Didn't she mention it?"

"No," he said, trying to keep from snapping.

"Man, Wilder, if I'd had that woman in my home, I'd have been there every night. She could work as hard as she wanted on her profession and I'd be the happiest guinea pig you ever saw."

"You have half of that right," Wilder growled. "We're just not sure guinea is the right type of pig."

"Stop sniping at each other," his mother stated calmly. "You're best friends, not little kids." But the look on her face showed that she was more than pleased that Wilder had snapped. If he guessed right, she wanted him to think of Virginia as marriageable.

He refused to do so.

She wasn't the right woman for him. No one was.

Liar.

After dessert and coffee, a large man with a florid complexion stepped to the microphone and began the ceremonies. First he introduced his students to the audience. It was obvious that Virginia was his prize pupil. Wilder watched her carefully, noticing that after her first sign of recognition and a flash of that beautiful smile in their direction, she kept her wide eyes glued on her mentor.

Charlie Feather introduced the esteemed guests—chefs and restaurant owners of some of the finest restaurants around the country, from California to Connecticut. As the ceremonies went on, it slowly sank into Wilder's head that Virginia was the diva of the cooking school and that she was being scouted by these honchos of the restaurant world.

When the ceremonies were over, several restaurateurs introduced themselves to Wilder, separating him from his tablemates. One woman who owned a restaurant in Los Angeles was obviously taken with him, telling him she used his computers for all her work, both business and personal. As she left, she handed him her card. "Come in for a free meal. Anytime," she said. Then she sauntered off, a swing in her hips meant to catch the attention of any full-blooded male. It certainly caught his friend's eye.

"Well, well, Wilder, you've got them coming and going, don't you?" Pete whispered.

"I don't know what you mean."

"Well, you'd better catch on soon. You're missing your own boat." Pete turned and walked away—directly toward Virginia. In a minute he was engaged in conversation with her and another female graduate.

"I've got to go," Wilder told his mother tersely.

She looked up in surprise. "You're not staying?"

"No. I have an appointment." Anything to get out of here. Anything to end the pain that was cutting through him right this minute. Anything not to see Pete and Virginia touching, hugging, laughing. "Sammy will take you home. I'll see you later."

"I thought I taught you better than that," his mother said slowly.

"You did. I just choose to ignore it right now." He kissed the top of her head. "I'm a big boy now, Mom, all grown up."

He strode off, but his mother's last barb caught up with him. "Well, I would have thought so, except that you keep proving otherwise."

He kept walking, wondering what in the hell was the matter with him. He had an urge so strong it took everything he had not to follow through. He wanted to sling Virginia over his shoulder caveman fashion and take her out of here. He wanted to make love to her in the darkness as if she would never leave him. He wanted to brand her as his very own.

It didn't make any difference to him that she had other plans for her life, and that his needs weren't important....

WHEN VIRGINIA DROVE UP to the house on Lick Creek, she was exhausted but still excited. She'd been offered a plum of a job and couldn't believe her luck. She'd known she was good at her craft, but if it hadn't been for Charlie's faith in her she might never have known just how much others in the business thought of her talents.

After the ceremonies, Charlie had introduced her to several of his guests, and the talk had led into offers she hadn't even dreamed of. The one she wanted most was the last. A hotel in Dallas with a five-star restaurant was looking for a middle chef.

At long last, she'd found her way to Mrs. Hunnicut and Pete. She'd seen Wilder leave, and her heart, buoyant and high with the expectation of sharing her good fortune with him, had plummeted.

But her pride was intact. She refused to ask where he'd gone and no one volunteered the information. Mrs. Hunnicut was proud and excited for her; Pete wanted to take her out to celebrate.

She said no to Pete and gave Mrs. Hunnicut's weathered cheek a kiss. "Thank you" she'd whispered. The card the woman had given her held enough cash that Virginia could move wherever she wanted without worrying about finances.

When Pete went to the bar to order another drink, Virginia sat next to Mrs. Hunnicut. "It's too much," she protested quietly. "This is more than any bonus should be."

Wilder's mother patted her hand. "You're quite right. That's why it's not a bonus, it's a gift." She tilted Virginia's chin to stare her square in the eye. "I don't have a daughter, but if I did, I would hope she'd be just like you. You're the kind of woman any mother would be proud of. You have depth and character, Virginia, and I admire that in anyone, especially in a woman who's had to make her own way."

Tears came to Virginia's eyes and she blinked quickly to keep them at bay. "Thank you. I don't know what I've done to earn such a wonderful friend, but thank you."

"You're welcome." Mrs. Hunnicut stood, testing her hip and leg before stepping away from the table. "And now, let's go home."

"You go on. I've got to stay awhile and help clean up."

"Wilder had an appointment," Mrs. Hunnicut said. "He won't be home until later." Wilder's mother seemed to have the ability to see straight through her.

Virginia sighed, her shoulders slumping. What was the use in hiding her feelings? It was almost over. "I guessed as much."

"I'm sorry."

"So am I." She stood and gave the older woman a hug. "Thank you again. I'll be leaving early in the morning."

"Where are you going?"

"I've been offered a position in Dallas. The hotel will put me up while I look for a place. I'll start work next week."

"In that case, send me your address as soon as you get settled. I expect long letters telling me what is going on in your life." Mrs. Hunnicut placed her purse strap over her arm. "Meanwhile, I'll see you in the morning." She rose and with slow, even steps, walked through the door, then disappeared down the hallway.

"Where did Mrs. Hunnicut go?" Pete asked, coming up behind Virginia. He had two glasses of champagne.

Virginia took a glass and practically downed it in three gulps. "Home," she said, sounding more like a small child than a woman fully grown. She *felt* like a small child, wanting the comfort of someone who cared for her. "Pete? Take me somewhere, will you? Somewhere there's a lot of people who don't know either one of us."

Pete's teasing look was transformed. He smiled into her eyes. "You've asked the right person. Let's go."

Taking her arm after setting down their champagne glasses, he led her out of the room and down the stairs. They stepped into his BMW, leaving her jalopy parked on the street.

Pete drove to Sixth Street, where the sidewalks were

filled with tourists and fun-lovers and they strolled among them, listening to the music that filtered through open doors. Jazz, rock and roll, rhythm and blues—it all poured forth from local bands hoping to make it big. The two of them stopped at one corner store and Pete bought Virginia a double-dip chocolate ice-cream cone. He chose praline. They strolled some more.

Virginia was filled with so many mixed feelings she barely said more than ten words. Pete was kind enough to honor her silence—for a while.

Finally he spoke. "Are your emotions tied up elsewhere?"

She didn't know what to say, so she told the truth. "Yes."

"I see," he said slowly. "And does that person feel the same way?"

It hurt to voice the answer, and she bit her lip before she finally blurted out, "No."

"Is it Wilder?"

Virginia withdrew even more. "This isn't a court of law, is it?"

"No." Pete touched the small of her back as if to reassure her. "I'm very interested in you, but I certainly wouldn't want to put you in a tough spot." They strolled down the block a ways before stopping and looking at a window display that had T-shirts with funny slogans printed on them. But Pete wasn't interested in any of that. "I know you'll probably be moving on in the next week or so, but I want you to know that if you're ever interested in seeing me, just call and let me know. Wherever you are, I'll be there."

"Pete..." Virginia began.

He placed his finger on her lips and gave a lopsided smile. "No, don't say no right now. Just keep the thought in mind, and anytime you need a male friend, I'm available."

With gentleness, Pete touched her mouth with his own. It was a sweet kiss. It was a compliment to her and she used it as a salve for her battered heart.

"Thank you," she said softly. "I only wish..." She stopped. No more wishes. She'd done enough damage by not thinking them through.

"Don't worry. My heart's intact, although my ego's a little bruised." He put his arm around her waist and they turned to walk toward the car. "But I'll manage to bounce back," he promised, a chuckle in his voice.

"It's nice to know I can be so easily forgotten," she retorted, but she was relieved. She didn't want Pete to be hurting because of *her* stupid wish.

It was after one in the morning when she got home. Pete had taken her back to her car, and they'd talked for another half an hour, discussing everything except his best friend and the state of her heart.

The house was dark. Virginia slipped upstairs, but she was too tense to sleep. Instead, she quickly began packing. It didn't take long. What wouldn't fit into her car could be sent at a later date.

Feeling anxious, Virginia slipped into her white satin gown and sat on the deck outside her room until dawn peeped over the canyon wall. Only then did she fall asleep for a few hours, before loading her car and taking off for Dallas.

According to Mrs. Hunnicut, Wilder wasn't home. "I don't know where he is," she said worriedly. "He's never disappeared without letting someone know before."

"Always the responsible one?" Virginia said sarcastically. But she knew he *was* responsible. He'd been the one to make sure his appointments were on time and that his mother was taken care of properly. He'd been the one to insist on protection when they made love. It had been Virginia who had irresponsibly given her heart to the wrong man.

"Yes. Always responsible," agreed Wilder's mother. "Sometimes I fretted that he'd never do something spur-of-the-moment. But now that he's done it, I'm not so sure I like it."

"I'm certain he's fine," Virginia assured her. "He's a big boy, Mrs. Hunnicut. If you hadn't been here, you never would have known he'd spent the night out."

The older woman's eyes were steady. "And neither would you."

Virginia's smile didn't reach her eyes. "I've enjoyed meeting you so much. Thank you for all your help and support." She bent down and gave her a warm hug. "Please take care."

"I will. And I guess you're right. My son is grown up and doesn't need his mother underfoot. He has a life of his own to lead."

She left Mrs. Hunnicut with a promise to write, then fled the house as if she couldn't wait for Dallas to appear on the horizon. It was just as well. It was hard to keep the tears from spilling.

All the way up Interstate 35, she cried.

All the way to the hotel, she cried.

All the way to her room, she cried.

By six the next morning, she'd stopped crying. Then the anger began building.

"Damn you, Wilder Hunnicut!" she muttered, staring in the mirror at the dark circles under her eyes. "Why couldn't you let go and enjoy the life we might have had together?"

But recognizing she was angry didn't lessen the pain of heartache. She straightened her spine and left the empty room to attend a breakfast with the director of the hotel.

WILDER SAT IN HIS OFFICE and stared out the window at the sunrise. In a few hours Virginia would leave for Dallas. Once she was gone, his weird mood would pass and his life would go on just as it had before she'd entered it. Things would be back to normal—including his emotions.

He could continue with his life, managing to live it as he saw fit, without the benefit of changing for someone else.

Without giving.

Without hurting.

Without loving.

Wilder watched the sun rise until heat shimmered on the buildings surrounding him. When the clock said noon, he left the office, drove home and went straight to bed. He slept all day, then went to a charity ball that night. He escorted Greta, who draped herself on his arm like a fluid anchor and looked like the sophisticated model she was. They met a hundred people in a room of a thousand. Too tired to go through the motions of being civil, he sent her home with Sammy.

When Wilder finally returned home, he poured a glass of wine, walked out to the deck and stared up at the moon—and then at the balcony just above him.

It was empty, no one there.

For the first time in his life, Wilder realized he'd lied to the one person he'd sworn always to tell the truth to—himself. Somehow along the line, he'd fallen in love. He didn't like it, didn't want to feel this way, wasn't sure what it meant. But lying was more painful than confronting those emotions. He knew he'd lied to himself long enough.

He loved Virginia.

Against all odds—her all-important career, her lack of social status, her lack of awe for him, her outrageous outspokenness—he loved her.

Moonlight spilled down on him, shimmering in the tears that ran down his face.

At that moment, Wilder was the loneliest man in the world.

Knowing look—they're thinking of Virginia, aren't
you?" he said.

"Yes." Her voice was unguarded. I he read the hurt
stare of unfair concern.

_____ 12 _____

WILDER DID THE ONLY THING he could do: he buried
himself in the business. His days were hectic, his nights
filled with enough paperwork to choke the government. But all his frantic activity didn't work as well as
it was supposed to. Images of Virginia still flickered
across his mind like frames of a movie: Virginia
stretched out on the bed, standing on the deck, working at her desk, telling some story to his mother in the
dining room. He missed her so very much.

His mother said nothing. She just watched him with
a knowing look in her eyes that he didn't want to question. After two weeks of working frenzy, he decided to
do something different. He had to attend another big
event at the art museum. This time he called a woman
he'd met last week and asked her if he could escort her.
She was very flattered and said yes immediately. It
salved his ego, but didn't fill the emptiness in his heart.
If anything, he felt even more guilty, as if he was cheat-
ing on Virginia. He shook off the feeling. He couldn't
allow himself the luxury of wallowing in his own blue
funk; he was late. His date was waiting for him to pick
her up. And he didn't give a damn.

Instead of leaving, he finally confronted his mother's

knowing look. "You're thinking of Virginia, aren't you?" he said.

"Yes." Her voice was soft, but in it he heard the firm strike of bat against ball.

"Maybe we should bribe her into coming back by offering her our chef's position."

His mother shrugged. "Perhaps. But I'm not the one who's starving. You are."

Wilder stomped out the door, but instead of going toward the car, he walked around the house to the cliff above the creek.

With resignation, he admitted his mother was right. He was hungry for Virginia. Starving. He needed her touch, her closeness. Her love.

What was he doing, dating some woman he cared nothing about, when the one he loved was in Dallas? Hell, he hadn't even bothered to let Virginia know how he felt. He hadn't even given her a clue about his love for her, yet he had hoped—expected against all odds—that she would stay with him. What a damn coward.

Wilder couldn't go on this way. He wasn't eating right, sleeping right, thinking right. He knew he had to see her. He had to let her know just how much he cared. If he didn't tell her, he'd never know. Maybe what she really wanted, craved, needed was not that job but to return to him. Who knew?

Hell, he knew better than that. At one time she'd loved him. He'd seen it in her eyes, heard in her voice, felt it in each and every touch. Because of his own cowardice, he'd thrown that all away.

It was a long shot, but he wasn't going to get any closer to happiness unless he tried something different. It was time to grow up. He had to let her know he was man enough to want—need—her in his life.

Finally, he was man enough for her.

TWO EVENINGS LATER he stood at the entrance of an exclusive hotel in the Market Street area of downtown Dallas. Tourists and business people bustled through the lobby, and at the restaurant a number of well-dressed, hungry patrons waited in the posh bar.

Earlier, Wilder had had a dozen roses and a note to Virginia delivered to the kitchen. He'd written that he was in Dallas and wanted to see her tonight. She'd left a message with his secretary that he should be here at nine o'clock sharp. At least she hadn't turned him away. Not yet.

While waiting for his table, Wilder listened to a couple in the lounge talking about what great hors d'oeuvres the restaurant had. He felt a point of pride in their observation. That was Virginia's doing.

As good as it was to hear the praise, it also made him realize that she'd already made a mark in just two weeks. How could he carry her out of here when she was just becoming the success they both knew she could be?

How could he live without her sensuous beauty, caring ways and wonderful sense of humor?

All the old doubts assailed him again. He couldn't ask her to be his wife when all she'd ever wanted and worked for was the chance to prove herself to the world.

A waiter tapped him on the shoulder. "Sir? Your table is ready. I'll freshen your drink and bring it to the table."

Once seated, the young man informed him that his dinner had already been chosen by the chef.

"I see. Do I get any input?"

"No, sir," the waiter said solemnly.

Hors d'oeuvres were first—two that Wilder had never tasted before. One had a peanut dip, the other a marinera sauce. Both were delicious.

Wilder kept his eyes on the kitchen area, but he didn't spot Virginia. Was she going to ply him with great food, but never confront him face-to-face? Tension built as her absence continued.

Her not meeting him would be more of a put-down than he could have imagined. It would be her way of saying that she'd give the same great meal to any past employer who happened to be in town. No emotion, no nothing except the barest courtesy.

Pork-loin medallions and a spiced pear dessert followed. Everything was delicious, the waiter was quiet and the wine was exactly right. Wilder was being treated like an honored guest, only there was no honored hostess.

Over his coffee, he started becoming annoyed. She'd ignored him long enough. Either she came out or he was going into the kitchen after her. With his mind made up, he took one last sip of his coffee.

The waiter appeared at his side. "Sir? The chef sends you this." He handed Wilder a note.

He opened it carefully, almost afraid of what he would find. Relief surged through him as he read it. She'd written, "If you wait for me, I'll join you."

His stomach clenched, then relaxed. "Tell her I'll be here," he said to the waiter.

Then he prayed as he'd never prayed before....

When she stepped out of the kitchen, he noticed she was much thinner than she'd been a little over two weeks ago, when she'd left Austin. Instead of making her look bad, gauntness accentuated her fine bone structure and wide eyes. He stood, greeting her with a light kiss and wishing he could take her in his arms instead. She pulled away from him before he could embrace her, silently warning him to keep his distance.

After he pulled out her chair, Virginia sat with quiet determination etched in her eyes. The waiter hurried over with coffee.

"How are you doing?" Wilder asked. "You look tired."

"Thanks," she stated warily. "It must be the weather. So do you."

"I missed you," he said simply.

She ignored those words. "Why the flowers?"

"Because you deserve them and I never gave them to you when I had the chance."

"And the visit?"

"I was in the area and just wanted to see how you were doing," he lied. She wasn't going to give him an inch. Suddenly he was scared. More scared than he'd ever been in his life.

"And have you found the woman of your dreams yet?" she asked.

"Yes. Have you found the man of your dreams yet?"

"Yes."

He'd gotten the answer he'd dreaded. She'd found someone else and there was no way she'd be with him. The ache in the pit of his stomach twisted into a stabbing pain.

"Is it Pete?"

"No."

"Whatever—both of us should receive congratulations," he said bitterly. "At least we've both found what we want. I only hope it brings you happiness."

"It will eventually," she said, her voice hollow and dull. Her gaze dropped to his plate. "Did you enjoy your meal?"

"It was wonderful. Fit for a king."

"I'm glad. It's on the house."

"I guess coming back to Lick Creek with me is out of the question?" he asked, smile playing around the corners of his mouth.

"For what, Wilder? What would I do if I went back with you?"

He didn't have the answer she wanted, and he knew it. All he could do was bluff his way through. "You could cook."

"Thanks. But I had a different audience in mind."

"I can find a job for you anywhere you want."

Her chin lifted. "I can find my own job anywhere I want."

"What do you want from me, Virginia?" he asked, leaning forward, wanting her to give him the answer he needed to hear. "Tell me, and I'll tell you if I can give it. Go ahead. Tell me."

Virginia stood, looking at him with all the sadness of the world in her eyes. "If I have to tell you, Wilder, it's not worth asking for." She tapped her fingers on the table, stalling for a moment. "I have to get back to the kitchen. Please tell your mother I miss her and that I hope she's feeling better."

"She's all packed up and moving back home next week. She's dying to be closer to her bridge group, to say nothing of her beloved bookstores," Wilder said, stalling their inevitable parting. "She said to tell you to come visit."

Virginia's smile was short. "Maybe."

He didn't want her to go, to leave him here. He knew very well what would come next—a hurt that couldn't be assuaged. Then, when the hurt finally dulled into an everyday ache, he would feel the unbelievable loneliness. That never dulled. "May I drive you home?"

"No, thanks." Suddenly Virginia leaned down and kissed him lightly on the lips. Her mouth brushing his was like a touch of sunlight. Before he could reach for her, she stood straight again and moved away. "Take care, Wilder," she said. "Have a good life."

And then she was gone.

Wilder sat quietly, staring at the space that had held

Virginia just moments ago. He could feel his heart breaking. He'd lost her because he'd found out too late that he loved her.

Wearily, he stood and walked out. It was time to go home. He had the rest of his life to feel sorry for himself.

IN THE MIDDLE of the night, Virginia carefully unpacked the old lamp. Everything else in the apartment was brand-new and shiny.

She stared at the lamp as it rested in the palm of her hand. She'd goofed on the second wish. She had to make this last one right. As much as she hurt for Wilder, she also knew he had to find his own happiness. And he'd never be happy until he loved a woman enough that he was willing to break down those impenetrable walls of his.

As of today she was resigned to losing Wilder, the man she loved, and so she made her last wish.

"May Wilder Hunnicut find the right woman to give him happiness, the woman upon whom he can bestow all his love and then receive love in return, the woman who will give him enough courage to break down his walls, the woman who will ensure that he lives happily ever after."

Wilder deserved it. He'd made Virginia's own life so bright and happy and real. She had graduated from cooking school with honors, she had a wonderful job doing what she wanted to do. And she'd even made good friends that she'd treasure for the rest of her life.

Lucky her.

Then, with sobs that racked her body, she cried herself to sleep.

VIRGINIA HAD NEVER WORKED so hard in her life, and she knew why she was doing it. She was using work as an excuse not to think of Wilder. She was successful—to an extent.

She couldn't control her sleeping hours, when he would show up in loving color in her dreams. Her nightime Romeo was funny, wise, sexy and, most of all, in love with her.

But she wasn't quite taken in by him. Daytime instantly brought reality back with a depressing bang.

Two weeks after Wilder's visit, Virginia was asked to submit menu choices for a very important private party. It was the first time she'd been chosen for such an honor and that bubble of excitement she'd lost on leaving Austin returned.

She spent three days working out the menu. Two days later, a memo in her mailbox told her the menu had been accepted and that she should continue preparing for the party, which was five days away. Pleasure bubbled through her. She got to do it all. She'd buy the produce, choose her helpers and prepare *everything*. It was the first big step she'd taken in her job, and she was ready for it. Finally, she'd be able to show her stuff. Many items on the menu were from recipes she'd created herself. Until now, she hadn't made them for anyone except the Hunnicuts and guests at her graduation dinner.

The night of the party was hectic. Virginia was pleasantly surprised that everything was going so smoothly. All the food was out and the waiters were doing their jobs. The clean-up crew was busy washing pots and pans. Virginia slipped into the back room, a small seated area where employees came to rest their tired bodies.

And for Virginia, there was always a letdown after the frantic hurriedness of cooking.

She wished she could have shared her excitement tonight with Wilder. She wished he could have enjoyed her menu, realized her talent and told her how good she was. She wished she could curl into his arms while he used all the words in the dictionary to tell her how wonderful she was. She wished...

"If wishes were horses, beggars would ride," she muttered, disgusted with her own thoughts.

"If that was the case, I'd be even more miserable. I'm not fond of horses," said a soft voice.

Wilder. Virginia turned slowly to confront the man who ruled her thoughts. He stood, hands in his pockets, staring down at her as if she were dessert. He was dressed in a fashionable tuxedo and looking like a million dollars. "What are you doing here?" she blurted out.

"It's my mother's party for some old Dallas friends. And you've done a wonderful job!" He grinned, not in the least apologetic for his lie by omission. "It was the only way I could get to see you again. And I needed to see you more than I needed to breathe."

It took a moment for Virginia to pull herself together. "You certainly have a funny way of showing your devotion."

"That's my point, exactly. I don't have *any* way of showing it. I don't know how." He was standing at least three feet away, but Virginia felt as if he was touching her. In a low voice thick with emotion, he said, "Show me how. Teach me."

"You don't know what you're saying."

He laughed derisively. "Oh yes I do. I'm asking you to rescue me from a fate worse than death."

"Which is?"

"Living without you."

Virginia gave Wilder a disbelieving look. "You're just full of it, aren't you?"

Her comment didn't faze him. "If you're talking about love, the answer is yes. I love you, Virginia Gallagher. I need you in my life. I need you in my heart. Please come back to me."

Her eyes widened. She told her heart to calm down, to stop beating erratically. This was just an illusion, only a dream. If he'd have been making a real declaration, he'd have had her in his arms. "Is this a joke?" she demanded.

"I've never been more serious," Wilder said.

She felt confused, disoriented. "Why now? Where were these wonderful declarations of love when I was in Austin with you? When I told you I was leaving? At my graduation?"

"I was running scared," Wilder admitted. "I didn't know which way to turn to get away from the torture you were putting me through."

"You were putting yourself through," she corrected. "I wasn't doing a thing."

Wilder didn't deny it. "I know. But I've always been organized and in control, in charge of my life. I never had to explain anything to anyone. Then you came along and all that changed. I worried about how to see you, when to see you, if I could see you. I lost track of things...hell, I missed important meetings! All because I was thinking about you." He came closer and hunkered down by her chair. His face was so close, his gaze so intense that she felt heat coming off him in waves. "I resented not being in control," he continued, on a roll. "I resented your intrusion into my private thoughts. I didn't know what to do, so I backed off."

Virginia cleared her throat. "That's one way to cope with love, I suppose. Then again, you could always just face it."

"I know that now," he admitted. "But I had to learn it the hard way—by losing you."

"I..." she couldn't talk. She couldn't think. Her gaze focused on his firm lips.

He placed two fingers over her mouth. "Don't say anything unless you're going to tell me you love me."

Virginia took a deep breath, full of relief. *That* was easy. "I love you," she said in a husky whisper.

A little of the tension left Wilder's body. "And I love you. With everything I've got, I love you. Please marry me and bring back my happiness. Please come to Austin and be with me."

Virginia had never seen Wilder this way. She'd bet her last dollar he'd never pleaded with anyone before which made his words even more powerful.

There was no hesitation in her heart, when she said, "Yes." Wilder's side was where she wanted to be.

His kiss was full of pent-up love. He covered her mouth with his, breathing his feelings right into her heart. He held her head between his hands as if she were his lifeline. His tongue pillaged her willing mouth.

When he pulled away, Virginia had to catch her breath. Her head swirled from the craziness of all this. She'd wished for it, but she'd never dreamed her wish would come true. "I guess you know what you're doing."

"I haven't a clue," he murmured, slowly sprinkling kisses on her cheeks, her forehead, her neck.

"You *do* know that I'm not going to be content to sit home and be the CEO's wife. I've trained for too long to be a chef to shelve that dream."

"I should have known," he said dryly, but with a smile on his face, "that you would refuse to give up your career for a man."

She still felt the sting of his words, though, and needed the reassurance of no more questions. "Would you do it for a woman?"

"No," he said firmly. "Neither one of us will give up anything. I was just teasing, darlin'. I don't want you to change for me, I want you to be with me."

A slow smile filled her eyes as happiness filled her heart. "Then you're in luck, big boy. Because under the conditions stated herewith, I accept your offer. I'm yours."

Wilder's laugh came from deep in his chest and filled the air with the sound of happiness, then he said, "And I'm yours. Don't you forget it."

Virginia felt a bubble of laughter moving up from her breast. "Thank you, magic lamp," she whispered before snuggling into his arms.

"Thank *you*, Virginia," he answered.

_____Epilogue_____

MRS. AMELIA WORTHIER leaned over the table to get another hors d'oeuvre. "These are so delicious," she said. "I don't know how you can stay away from them."

Ila Hunnicut smiled. "I've had too many already. My daughter-in-law created them, you know."

"Your daughter-in-law? I didn't know Wilder had married! That's the kind of news one should share with the bridge club, you know."

"Well, he just proposed," Ila stated in her own defense, glancing at her watch.

"How wonderful for you!" Amelia exclaimed. "Do you like her?"

"Of course I like her." Ila carefully chose another hors d'oeuvre. "I chose her, didn't I?"

Amelia looked blankly at her longtime friend. "You _chose_ her? Wilder let you choose his bride?"

"Yes. But Wilder doesn't know. And neither does she," Ila confided. "But you can't leave important things like this up to young people or they'll never get around to it. So I...arranged it."

"But how?"

"Do you remember a woman we used to see at the bookstore? Her name was Sadie."

Amelia's forehead wrinkled. "Vaguely."

"Well, her daughter was a social climber, but Sadie is down-to-earth, with a great **deal** of common sense. We used to meet occasionally for lunch and talk about our children. Then one day she told me she knew a girl I might be interested in meeting, for Wilder. I watched her for a while and decided Sadie was right on target."

"But does Wilder love her?"

"Just as much as his father loved me. And that was enough to take the starch out of my husband's shirts, thank goodness. I gave him all the happiness he ever wanted. I want Wilder to have that, too."

"Well, goodness only knows, he's certainly the catch of the century." Amelia Worthier frowned. "You didn't use that ploy with the lamp again, did you? I seem to remember that you convinced your husband it was magic."

"And it still is," Mrs. Hunnicut said with conviction. "Aren't miracles lovely?"

"You sly fox, you. Are you going to give it to her to wish on?"

"Already did." Ila chuckled. "And I'm pretty sure she's used up all her wishes. Now the Hunnicuts are on their own." She sat back and smiled contentedly.

COMING NEXT MONTH

#637 BRIDE OVERBOARD Heather MacAllister
Brides on the Run, Book II

Blair Thomason was going to take the plunge—into marriage, that is. But when she found herself on a yacht, about to marry a crook, she did the only thing she could—she jumped. Lucky for Blair, gorgeous Drake O'Keefe was there to pull her out of the Gulf. Except she'd barely escaped marrying one man, only to be stranded with another!

#638 ROARKE: THE ADVENTURER JoAnn Ross
New Orleans Knights, Book I

For journalist Roarke O'Malley rescuing a beautiful, sexy woman was second nature. But he knew better than to fall in love, especially with a woman who couldn't remember her past. Still, he couldn't abandon Daria Shea to the men who were determined to harm her. Too late he realized the greatest danger was losing his heart....

#639 RESTLESS NIGHTS Tiffany White
Blaze

Victoria Stone's erotic daydreams about a sexy gunslinger were harmless enough, until Zack DeLuca came along. Not even in her wildest imaginings had Victoria pictured herself responding so brazenly to a perfect stranger. And it was completely crazy to let him take her to a ghost town where all her fantasies were far too real....

#640 THE RETURN OF DANIEL'S FATHER Janice Kaiser

Ethan Mills was back and determined to claim his only son, little Daniel. One woman—and the wrath of a town—stood in his way. But Kate Rawley was soon defenseless in the face of Ethan's unyielding love for his child...and his overwhelming sexuality.

AVAILABLE NOW:

#633 THE GETAWAY BRIDE
Gina Wilkins

#634 WISHES
Rita Clay Estrada

#635 THE BLACK SHEEP
Carolyn Andrews

#636 RESCUING CHRISTINE
Alyssa Dean

Take 4 bestselling love stories FREE

Plus get a FREE surprise gift!

Special Limited-time Offer

Mail to Harlequin Reader Service®

3010 Walden Avenue
P.O. Box 1867
Buffalo, N.Y. 14240-1867

YES! Please send me 4 free Harlequin Temptation® novels and my free surprise gift. Then send me 4 brand-new novels every month, which I will receive before they appear in bookstores. Bill me at the low price of $2.90 each plus 25¢ delivery and applicable sales tax, if any.* That's the complete price and a savings of over 10% off the cover prices—quite a bargain! I understand that accepting the books and gift places me under no obligation ever to buy any books. I can always return a shipment and cancel at any time. Even if I never buy another book from Harlequin, the 4 free books and the surprise gift are mine to keep forever.

142 BPA ASJP

Name	(PLEASE PRINT)	
Address	Apt. No.	
City	State	Zip

This offer is limited to one order per household and not valid to present Harlequin Temptation® subscribers. *Terms and prices are subject to change without notice. Sales tax applicable in N.Y.

UTEMP-693   ©1990 Harlequin Enterprises Limited

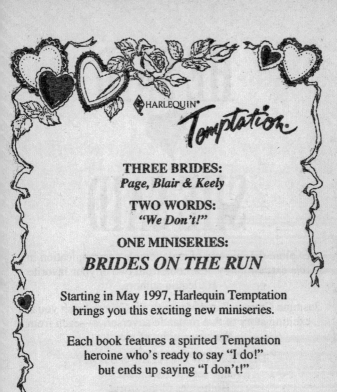

HARLEQUIN® *Temptation*

THREE BRIDES:
Page, Blair & Keely

TWO WORDS:
"We Don't!"

ONE MINISERIES:

BRIDES ON THE RUN

Starting in May 1997, Harlequin Temptation
brings you this exciting new miniseries.

Each book features a spirited Temptation
heroine who's ready to say "I do!"
but ends up saying "I don't!"

Watch for these special books:

#633 THE GETAWAY BRIDE
by Gina Wilkins, May 1997
#637 BRIDE OVERBOARD
by Heather MacAllister, June 1997
#641 NOT THIS GAL!
by Glenda Sanders, July 1997

Available wherever Harlequin books are sold.

HE SAID

♥

SHE SAID

Explore the mystery of male/female communication in
this extraordinary new book from two of your favorite
Harlequin authors.

Jasmine Cresswell and Margaret St. George bring you the
exciting story of two romantic adversaries—each from
their own point of view!

DEV'S STORY. CATHY'S STORY.
As he sees it. As she sees it.
Both sides of the story!

The heat is definitely on, and these two can't stay out of
the kitchen!

Don't miss **HE SAID, SHE SAID.**
Available in July wherever Harlequin books are sold.

And the Winner Is...
You!

...when you pick up these great titles
from our new promotion at your
favorite retail outlet this June!

Diana Palmer
The Case of the Mesmerizing Boss

Betty Neels
The Convenient Wife

Annette Broadrick
Irresistible

Emma Darcy
A Wedding to Remember

Rachel Lee
Lost Warriors

Marie Ferrarella
Father Goose

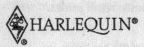 

Look us up on-line at: http://www.romance.net ATWI397-R

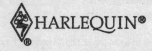

On the plus side, you've raised a
wonderful, strong-willed daughter.
On the minus side, she's using that
determination to find

A Match For
MOM

Three very different stories of mothers,
daughters and heroes...from three of your
all-time favorite authors:

GUILTY
by Anne Mather

A MAN FOR MOM
by Linda Randall Wisdom

THE FIX-IT MAN
by Vicki Lewis Thompson

Available this May wherever
Harlequin and Silhouette books are sold.

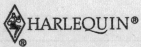 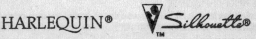

HREQ597

As Seen on TV!

Free Gift Offer

With a Free Gift proof-of-purchase
from any Harlequin® book, you can receive
a beautiful cubic zirconia pendant.

This stunning marquise-shaped stone is a genuine cubic
zirconia—accented by an 18" gold tone necklace.
(Approximate retail value $19.95)

Send for yours today...
compliments of ◈HARLEQUIN®

To receive your free gift, a cubic zirconia pendant, send us one original proof-of-purchase, photocopies not accepted, from the back of any Harlequin Romance®, Harlequin Presents®, Harlequin Temptation®, Harlequin Superromance®, Harlequin Intrigue®, Harlequin American Romance®, or Harlequin Historicals® title available at your favorite retail outlet, together with the Free Gift Certificate, plus a check or money order for $1.65 U.S./$2.15 CAN. (do not send cash) to cover postage and handling, payable to Harlequin Free Gift Offer. We will send you the specified gift. Allow 6 to 8 weeks for delivery. Offer good until December 31, 1997, or while quantities last. Offer valid in the U.S. and Canada only.

Free Gift Certificate

Name: _____

Address: _____

City: _____ State/Province: _____ Zip/Postal Code: _____

Mail this certificate, one proof-of-purchase and a check or money order for postage and handling to: HARLEQUIN FREE GIFT OFFER 1997. In the U.S.: 3010 Walden Avenue, P.O. Box 9071, Buffalo NY 14269-9057. In Canada: P.O. Box 604, Fort Erie, Ontario L2Z 5X3.

FREE GIFT OFFER
ONE PROOF-OF-PURCHASE

084-KEZ

To collect your fabulous FREE GIFT, a cubic zirconia pendant, you must include this original proof-of-purchase for each gift with the properly completed Free Gift Certificate.

084-KEZR